A WIND UP THE WILLOW

for Jenny

Other books by the same author

Stage plays
Wheelchair Willie
Skoolplay
Panic

Television plays
Rotten
Bobby Dazzler
Happy Families

Screenplays
Brown Ale with Gertie
O'Connor

A WIND UP THE WILLOW

Alan Brown

JOHN CALDER · LONDON
RIVERRUN PRESS INC. · NEW YORK

First published in Great Britain, 1980, by
John Calder (Publishers) Ltd.,
18 Brewer Street,
London W1R 4AS
and in the U.S.A., 1980, by
riverrun press Inc.,
175 Fifth Avenue,
New York NY 10010

Originally published in Great Britain, 1978, by
John Calder (Publishers) Ltd., in
New Writing and Writers 15

British Library Cataloguing in Publication Data
Brown, Alan, *b.1951*
   A wind up the willow. – (Riverrun writers).
   I. Title   II. Series
   823'.9'1F   PR6052.R587W/   79-41585
   ISBN 0-7145-3808-6

Photoset in 11/11pt Baskerville by Specialised Offset Services Ltd.,
Liverpool
Printed & bound by The Hunter Rose Company Ltd., Toronto, Canada.

A WIND UP THE WILLOW

Wilf stared at the ball of mucus that rested on the tip of his finger.

'Little cunt.'

It had taken Wilf three-quarters of an hour to extract it and now he would be late for the office.

'Sod it.'

He stared out of the window and beheld the splendour of the Liverpool Anglican Cathedral.

He put the ball inside his mouth where it adhered to his palate.

Wilf was a well-worn fifty.

His face was lined.

His teeth were false.

His grubby grey suit hung limply on his flabby body.

'Only another eight hours,' he mused, 'and I shall become "The Bohemian".'

It was a case of walking to the office owing to lack of funds. It would be nine forty-five before he got there. He had been warned thirteen times already.

But they wouldn't sack him. Not Wilf.

His flat was right at the top. Not a flat. More of a glorified bed-sitter. Only four pounds a week.

He shut the door of his room behind him with an innermost feeling of despair.

He made for the broken toilet at the end of the corridor. He kicked a bucket filled with water.

'Grudge by name and grudge by nature,' he said.

What a name to be lumbered with. Wilfred Howard Grudge. Solicitor's clerk and part-time freak. Father confessor to Miss Chong.

Miss Chong. When would she learn to flush the toilet?

Wilf poured half the contents of the bucket down the pan

before he relieved himself.

'About time this bloody thing was fixed.'

For three seconds, Wilf thought he was the only English person in the world.

He often had such thoughts. Such thoughts disturbed him greatly.

Wilf and the bucket were empty.

What would Harvey say?

Probably out at court.

That was it. He would be out at court. Wilf was safe.

Outside, in the ethnic outside, Wilf felt the stares of the gaily dressed youngsters. He wished he were young.

He had an appointment with the doctor for that evening. Dr. Gwambi.

His piles were playing him up again. Piles. Piles of piles.

Down the hill into the city. Hotbed of commerce.

'I am Wilfred. Wilfred Grudge. Wilfred Howard Grudge. And I am a well-worn fifty. Solicitor's clerk. Harvey's clerk.'

Wilf nudged himself through the collection of delivery boys that had congregated outside the office building door. The lift was coming down. He watched, sweat forming on his wrinkly brow. The light above the door signalled the descent.

Clunk.

The doors opened.

Wilf held his breath.

Harvey.

The tall, smart figure, holding briefcase and wearing all black apart from an immaculate white shirt, stared at the dishevelled, perspiring mess.

'Morning, Mr. Harvey.'

His voice was high-pitched. The voice of a pantomime character.

Wilf's scrotum was being dragged inside out.

The situation had occurred several million times before. Why was this time so different? At fifty it would be difficult finding another job. He couldn't make a living as a full-time Bohemian.

Mr. Harvey looked at the gold watch that adorned his tanned wrist, sniffed, and pushed past Wilf.

'Be at the Crown Court at ten o'clock. I'll need you to take notes,' he commanded.

When it was safe to do so, Wilf made a rude sign.

A delivery boy shouted, 'You should have seen what he just done, mate!' to Harvey.

And Wilf felt the familiar wave of depression, like cold and dirty bathwater, surging.

W.H. Grudge. Legal executive. Something in the city. Twenty quid a week. The part-time tea woman earned that.

Wilf got in the lift and pressed a button.

The top floor. Room at the top.

Wilf felt, vaguely, like masturbating. But there was no real point so early in the morning.

Lunchtime was the best when the girls, the little office girls, spent their luncheon vouchers.

'Morning, Wilf,' chirped Valerie, as the doors opened.

Wilf grimaced. Harvey had told them all that he was to be called Mr. Grudge. They all did when Harvey was around. He pretended not to hear her.

Valerie stepped in as Wilf stepped out. Her arms were folded across her breasts and her head was snugly buried in her shoulders. A cosy person.

'What's the matter with you, then?' she enquired cheekily.

Harvey's secretary should have more dignity. More aplomb.

Wilf grunted. Valerie shrugged.

The place was dark, dismal, Dickensian. Dust and corruption. The laughter of tarty young females, paid the bare minimum, came from the filing room. He had to go in there to sign the book. Harvey's signing-in book.

'Sod it.'

Wilf used the other entrance to his office.

Bernard jumped up as Wilf walked in, and tried desperately to conceal a motorbike magazine. Then he breathed a sigh of relief. 'Aww, it's only you. I thought it was Harvey.'

'What are you doing? Get on with your work,' said Wilf.

Bernard was only sixteen but had big muscles and, deep down, Wilf was frightened of him.

Bernard nonchalantly scraped green stuff from his teeth and said, 'What was that, old Grudgey, Grudgey, Grudgey?' He pushed Wilf's shoulder. 'Old Grudgey,

Grudgey, Grudgey.'
Four females entered the room to watch the event.
'You must have some work to do. I've got to be at Court in
five minutes,' said Wilf.
'Old Grudgetty Grudgetty Grooo.' Bernard pushed again
and Wilf hit the wall.
'Get 'im, Bern,' said one of the girls.
'Dirty old get,' said another.
'Have you seen the way he looks at yer,' said yet another.
Wilf felt something flowing and presumed it to be
adrenalin.
'Stop this at once or I shall fire you all!' Wilf could hardly
believe he'd said it.
The youngsters stared at one another in silence. Then
Bernard said 'You'll what?'
'Fire you all ...'
There was a peal of laughter.
'It's you what's getting the boot, you dirty old get.'
Wilf recognized the girl as Maureen. A girl of eighteen who
worked the switchboard.
A nice looking girl.
Getting the boot.
'Valerie typed the letter to the lad who's getting your job.
She said he's ever so good looking.'
The room swam. Wilf swam in it. A huge hob-nailed boot
was hovering in mid-air.
The Boot.
Wilf fled from the room, scuttled along the corridor, and
arrived in Harvey's office. He fumbled through the letter
tray.
There it was.

> Mr. D. Heron,
> 56, Stagnation Crescent,
> Birkenhead.
>
> Dear Mr. Heron,
>   It is with pleasure that I confirm your appointment as
> clerk at a salary of £30 per week. Will you please report
> to this office ...

Wilf had seen enough. He tore the letter into shreds.
Back in the corridor, Wilf passed Wilson, the part-time,

semi-senile conveyancing clerk.

'Sorry to hear you're leaving us,' croaked Wilson.

Laughter was coming from young, fully-employed people.

'I am getting the sack. They are going to sack me.'

He fumbled in his pocket for his key to the toilet. Such pettiness.

He sniffed again.

Wilf went into the toilet.

Wilf locked himself in a cubicle.

Wilf made himself comfortable and took out his pencil.

> *Here I sit broken-hearted*
> *Spent a penny and only ...*

The lead broke.

Wilf heard someone else enter. He heard slightly asthmatic breathing.

'Grudge. Come on Grudgey. You should be at Court now.'

It was Bernard's voice.

'Not going,' said Wilf.

There was some clambering outside the w.c. door and Bernard's head appeared at the top of it.

'Come on, Wilf,' coaxed the younger.

Wilf looked up with such pathos in his face that Bernard guffawed loudly, fell, and broke two fingers. His shrieks of pain almost woke the dead.

Wilf pretended that nothing had happened.

Bernard staggered out, shrieking and searching for sympathy.

Poor, poor Wilf, thought Wilf.

'I wish Julian was here.'

Julian woke up.

On the white pillow he saw the black hairs that had fallen out whilst he slept.

His tongue explored the hole in his tooth where the filling had dropped out the day before.

His pink silk pyjamas glared at him and he felt ill. He closed his eyes again and went back to sleep.

Three minutes later he awoke. He could not remember the world he had just visited but he somehow knew it was not a good place.

He felt edgy and unsure.

He released a hissing, garlic fart and was disgusted.

His mild need-a-wee-wee erection was beginning to irritate.

Julian parted the silk and looked at his chest.

Julian wished he had more hairs on it.

He pressed a button and the blinds opened and the beautiful bedroom was flooded with morning light.

The day stretched out emptily before him. Soon he would be thirty. He felt heartily sick.

He thought of suicide, then he thought of bacon and eggs; he thought of becoming a Roman Catholic, then he thought of good strong coffee.

Julian scraped sleep from his eyes. He wished he hadn't argued with Malcolm.

Something soft was rubbing against him. He kicked it.

'Ouch!' said a girl.

Julian sat up.

'You're still here, lady of the red lamp,' he said.

'You bet I am,' said Deborah. 'You owe me seventy pounds.'

Her brown hair was unruly, her large breasts were white.

Julian kicked her again and again and again.

She said that he was hurting her, but refrain he did not.

Bruised, she leapt from the bed.

He held his head high. Dark-haired, white-skinned, tall and handsome with blue eyes that shone. He insulted her horribly.

'What do you think I am,' she whimpered. 'Aren't I a human being too?'

The poor girl received another kick, for Julian was now out of bed. He chased her and caught her and threw her down onto the floor.

'No. Don't tickle me ... PLEEEEEEEASE!!'

She begged and cringed.

Julian pinned her down and tickled and tickled.

She sobbed and giggled and slobbered and begged and probably would have died had the telephone not rung.

'Yes,' said Julian, panting.

'Hi, Ju. If you're doing nothing better, why not come for drinkies in twenty-three minutes?' The caller, who was Malcolm, hung up.

Julian smiled and felt better already.

On the floor, Deborah parted her bruised thighs and looked

very sexy.

Julian kicked her.

She started to cry.

'You bastard,' she sobbed. 'You bastard.'

'Oh, just make some coffee,' yawned Julian.

'Where's my seventy quid ...?'

'Make some coffee!'

Deborah put on her gown and then put on some coffee and Julian showered and deodorized.

Deborah gave him coffee and he drank it.

Then he got out his flick-knife and said, 'Now get out.'

Deborah looked down and through the semi-transparent nylon saw the dark triangle of her pudenda.

'But my money ...'

'Get out or I'll cut your nipples off.'

She knew that he meant it, so she gathered up her clothes, put on her shoes, and went to the door.

'Next time I see you,' she taunted, 'I'll remember to have a candle with me.' Her eyes were wet.

And she slammed the door behind her.

'Huh,' he said, and smiled strangely.

Julian put on his woodpecker suit and flew out of the door and down the stairs to where his Rolls Royce was parked. He never locked it.

Halfway along the Bayswater Road, he slotted his 'Obscenities' cassette into place. He turned up the volume.

Julian decided to stop at a red light. He pressed a button and the lid of the Rolls folded back. He felt the wind in his face. Fellow motorists and passers-by seemed disturbed.

The obscenities poured out alarmingly.

Whilst anonymous in his bird-suit, Julian was in a state of euphoria. Soon he would be with Malcolm.

The tamed brute of an engine purred.

Julian parked as well as he could outside the yellow mews house and flapped his wings and chirped.

Malcolm watched from a window.

Julian smiled and Malcolm smiled back.

Julian tried to balance on one leg on the front passenger seat of the Royce. He succeeded.

'Stop farting about out there and come in if you're coming!' called Malcolm.

Externally, Malcolm seemed a nice enough bloke, but

Julian knew better. That was why Julian had befriended him.

Julian flew inside and pecked Malcolm in the genital.

Julian smiled and said, 'Hello, little rattlesnake.'

Malcolm was relieved that things were back to normal.

'I say, Mal. Would you buzz my butler and ask him to cycle round here as fast as he can,' requested Julian.

'Sure, Ju. I'd do anything for you.'

Malcolm telephoned Sambo.

Julian sang an old Noel Coward song.

Then Julian and Malcolm proceeded to get drunk.

When Wilf decided he had better face up to things, it was half past ten. He went into the little room which was designated for the purposes of brewing and drinking tea. Nobody seemed to be about.

He watched the kettle boil.

He felt unhappy.

It was a hard life.

He made the tea. He was used to making tea. It came from years and years of solitary tea-making. Wilf was a very solitary man.

He sipped.

His hair was getting long. He fell between so many stools. He didn't belong anywhere. He was a wretch. Pathetic. Julian had said he was pathetic. It was not a nice word to use. Pathetic.

He was not pathetic.

He was not some grovelling little clerk.

He was "The Bohemian".

'Ha ha ha ha,' he laughed.

Julian had nicknamed him that. Julian was a good lad. A fine young man. If only Julian were with him now.

Valerie entered into the little room and said, 'You're for it now. Fancy breaking the little bugger's fingers.'

She sat beside him.

She always made a point of showing her wedding ring to him as soon as she came anywhere near. To let him know that she wasn't available to him. Wilf hadn't been near a woman for ten years and he wasn't going to start now.

'Wha'd'yemean?' he said, none too eloquently.

'Bernard said you broke his fingers because he called you

"Grudgey Groo".'
'What rubbish.'
Wilfred had been in his second year at college when Julian
was born. Wilf was of gentle birth. His parents had rejected
him when he had married Phoebe. The way Wilf had said,
'what rubbish', reminded him of his father. A father who,
against all odds, had managed to die a bankrupt. Wilf
wondered if his mother still lived.
'That's what he says,' said Valerie, pouring herself a cup of
tea.
Wilf stared at her menacingly. 'I've got a bone to pick with
you,' he said.
She scratched her thigh, revealing a clumsily stitched repair
in her tights. Wilf made a point of not staring.
'You mean that letter?'
'What else?' spat Wilf.
She gave a sexy wriggle. 'I thought you might have guessed
my feelings for you, you hunk,' and she pouted her lips and
narrowed her eyes.
'There was no need to tell all the juniors. And old Wilson.'
Valerie laughed.
Wilf knew he should be angry, but really he was incapable.
He was going to call her a bitch, but her husband was a
long-distance lorry driver and they were strong.
He finished his tea and wondered if the Court Case had
started.
He slunk out, leaving Valerie giggling and adjusting her
bra.

Julian was singing merrily.
Malcolm was vomiting slightly.
Sambo arrived, black and out of breath.
'Where have you been, you negro?' asked Julian.
'Sorry, but I was held up in Piccadilly. The lights were
against me all the way.'
Julian pecked him in the eye, causing it to bleed.
'No excuse,' said Malcolm. 'Blowed if I'd let my boy fob me
off like that.'
'Right,' said Julian.
The drunkards stood up and Sambo backed away.
'Come and get your medicine, blackie,' said Julian.
'Have mercy, Master Julian,' pleaded Sambo.

Julian's wing flashed down.
Sambo screamed.

Wilf, clutching his note pad under his arm, was trying to run. It was impossible.
His little legs had seen far better days, that was for sure. He gave it up and walked quickly in the direction of the Crown Court.
'Hello, Wilf.'
It was Brian. Wilf's friend.
Wilf said, 'Hello.'
'Haven't seen you for ages,' said Brian, who was now walking back towards the Court, trying to keep up with Wilf.
'Haven't you?' said Wilf.
Brian was a nice, lonely solicitor's clerk. They had met one day in a stationery shop. Afterwards, they had lunched on sausages and chips followed by apple crumble and custard and a cup of tea. Brian had offered Wilf a cigarette but Wilf had declined.
'Look,' said angst-ridden Wilf, 'I'll call you sometime.'
'You said that last time. That was six months ago.'
Wilf said, 'If you'll excuse me, I'm on a very important case.'
Wilf ran away.
Away from the Court and Brian.
He didn't really care and arrived, out of breath, at the Pier Head. He ambled along the pier.
Wilf had resigned himself to redundancy: He would steal all he could from Harvey.
The smell of the River Mersey drifted up to his nostrils.
Wilf.
Shabby. Downtrodden.
Walking alone. Thinking of petty crime.
He wondered why Julian hated him.
Wilf kicked a discarded Pepsi can. It rattled and clunked.
The weather was warm. A warm September mid-morning.
He had no money on him to buy anything. It was so humiliating. His money just seemed to disappear. It was too bad.
'We are the lost sheep,' said a voice in his head.
'We are indeed,' said Wilf. He said it in a loud voice and a

workman heard him and stared.

Wilf was conscious of smelling. He felt uncomfortable. He couldn't take his jacket off because of the coffee stain. What the hell. Wasn't he "The Bohemian"?

Wilf walked and sat down, walked and sat down. One o'clock found him in a large chain store.

He put his jacket back on to give himself an air of respectability, and browsed through the pens.

One of the closed circuit cameras was focussed on him. He could feel it staring.

He scratched his head and moved on.

He had been in the store every Monday for five years, except, of course, for holidays, etc. Every week he had managed to steal something. It didn't matter what it was. As long as he had managed to put one over on the Organization.

Wilf made his way to the haberdashery counter and scooped up a handful of buttons and put them in his pocket.

He was sweating.

His armpits were like swamps.

He was getting old. That explained it. He was getting long in the tooth.

Then he took three pairs of tights from a stand and stuffed them down his trousers.

What was happening? Why was he being so rash?

Quickly, he headed for the door.

Three yards outside the door a fresh-faced young man said, 'We have reason to believe that you have goods on your person for which you have not paid. Will you please accompany me to the office.'

A shiver ran down Wilf's back. His very entrails quivered.

He considered running, but that would be so undignified. He would bluff.

'Well done,' said Wilf, patting the young man on the shoulder. 'I shall make a full report to your manager. What is your name?'

'I am the manager,' said the young man in a tired voice. Wilf noticed black rings beneath his eyes. 'Please come into the office. We are causing an obstruction.'

Wilf went.

Julian stubbed a half-smoked cigar in an ashtray.

'Why do you think it is, Ju, that these blackies have white palms and soles?' Malcolm asked.

'No idea, darling,' answered Julian.

Sambo was strapped to Malcolm's bed, naked except for a leopard skin loincloth that they insisted he wore around the house.

'What shall we do to him today?' asked Malcolm.

Julian shrugged indifferently. 'I don't suppose he's bathed.'

Julian gave Sambo a peck on the nipple. Then Julian removed his feathery disguise.

'I think you'd look superb in a caterpillar outfit,' said Malcolm, and he pressed the ball of his thumb into Sambo's adam's apple. 'See to it.'

Sambo croaked.

Sambo was, amongst other things, responsible for Julian's wardrobe.

'My God, this is boring,' sighed Julian.

Julian stood naked above the prostrated figure. 'Open your mouth,' he snarled.

Wilf was feeling very lonely.

One of the shop girls brought him a cup of tea. It was so humiliating, sitting there, waiting for the police to arrive.

'Have you a toilet?' he asked the girl, 'I think I'm going to be sick.'

Julian looked disgusted.

Sambo choked and coughed.

Malcolm said,. 'You filthy wog. Look what you've done to my bed.'

'I really am sick and tired of all this,' said Julian.

Malcolm looked at him. Malcolm had bonde hair and was starting to go plump.

'It is a bit old hat,' Malcolm agreed.

Malcolm got his cine camera and a shining butcher's cleaver.

'I'll put some loud music on,' said Julian.

'Wagner would be super, love,' suggested Malcolm.

Sambo begged for mercy.

Malcolm asked Julian, 'Would you rather snip or snap?'

Sambo begged for mercy.

Julian turned irritably and smashed Sambo's jaw with the

blunt side of the cleaver.

'It does mean you won't get your caterpillar suit,' Malcolm pointed out.

Julian took a mouthful of gin and threw the bottle to the floor.

'Action!' he screamed.

Sambo tried to scream louder than the music but couldn't.

Malcolm zoomed in and out.

Julian chopped and hacked.

When Sambo was reduced to a bloody, scattered mess, Malcolm stopped the camera and stripped. He jumped onto the bed and said to Julian, 'Come on in, the gore is lovely.'

Julian jumped onto the bed and kissed Malcolm.

Malcolm ripped something from beneath a section of ribcage and handed it to Julian.

'I give you my heart,' said Malcolm.

Julian smiled.

Malcolm adjusted an arm and a section of leg, and lay back. 'You know,' he said thoughtfully, staring at the ceiling, 'you simply must have a caterpillar suit by next week.'

'Why next week?' asked a relaxing, over-exerted Julian.

'Because, you silly,' explained Malcolm, exploring Julian's anatomy, 'it's my birthday.'

They began to make love and became so engrossed that neither of them noticed Sambo's soul drift slowly away.

Wilf was breathing hard. He had managed to give them the slip. He looked over his shoulder and saw that no one was pursuing him.

He made a bee-line for the office.

'Mr. Harvey wants to see you as soon as you get back,' said Maureen.

Wilf stared at her.

'Better see what he wants, dirty old Grudgegrudge-grooooooooo.'

She ran away before Wilf could react, not that he would have.

Wilf walked along the cool passageway and knocked on the battered door.

'Come,' said Harvey's voice.

Wilf went in without changing his expression, and sat down at Harvey's request.

Wilf's employer was smiling benignly.

Wilf was blushing.

Wilf pushed hair from the side of his face and an avalanche of dandruff was released.

Wilf got fired.

Miss Plimsoll smiled warmly.

'I'm awfully sorry, but I'm afraid I can't order anything from you today,' she said to the sweet salesman.

'That's all right,' replied the sweet salesman, although it wasn't really.

But Miss Plimsoll seemed to bring out the gentility in everybody.

The salesman said, 'Cheerio, then,' and left.

And once again, Miss Plimsoll was alone in her little shop.

A shop in a less fashionable part of Chelsea.

Just a small tobacconist's which showed little profit but kept her happy enough and took up a large part of her spiritless life.

Miss Plimsoll straightened a chewing gum display and dusted a sherbert fountain with her spotless handkerchief.

She opened the till. It went 'ping'.

She had taken almost three pounds today.

In ten minutes she would make herself a cup of tea.

Miss Plimsoll was sixty eight. Her life was a long series of unselfish deeds and sacrifices. She had a ready smile and all her own teeth.

A fly buzzed above her head.

She said, 'Shoo.'

The door opened and a little boy came into the shop.

'Something for a penny, please,' he said.

Miss Plimsoll, who was still a virgin, gave a sigh.

Wilf was sorting out his desk. The amount of rubbish he had accumulated was amazing.

He felt quite light-hearted.

Bernard was watching him, his hand bandaged.

Wilf had enjoyed telling Harvey what to do with his job. One in the eye for old Harvey.

'I'm sorry,' said Bernard, thinking that his antics and

broken fingers were responsible for Wilf's dismissal. 'I'm sorry 'bout this, Mr. Grudge.'

Wilf said nothing. His jacket lay crumpled on the floor, and he was revealing the stain on his shirt. The odour of his body was becoming offensive.

Even the girls in the filing room were silent. Valerie was nowhere to be seen.

Harvey came into the office and said, 'We will send your cards to your home.' And then he said to Bernard, 'Come with me. I have a job for you.'

They went, leaving Wilf alone.

Wilf had meant to enquire as to his eligibility for holiday pay. But had been so concerned with looking like a martyr that he had forgotten all about it.

He had salvaged a few old pens and an old *Playboy* magazine. That was all there was of value.

'Pathetic,' he said, and tried to smile.

He thrust some divorce statements into his pocket. Some of them made interesting reading.

Then he walked out of the office for good.

Halfway down the passageway he remembered his jacket. 'Sod it,' he said.

When Wilf arrived at Canning Street he felt one hundred per cent happier. A millstone had been taken from around his neck.

He was back home and free.

He almost ran up the stairs.

His key eagerly entered his lock. He was safe once more.

He turned on his radio. Some kind of woman's programme hissed noisily from the cheap loudspeaker.

Wilf examined his larder. Nothing.

He had intended to pilfer some money from the cash box but events had deemed otherwise. He collapsed onto the bed and cupped his hands behind his head.

The room was dusty and shabby but Wilf didn't care. It was his retreat.

There was a knock on the door.

Wilf leapt up and said, 'Who is it?'

'Me.'

It was Miss Chong. What could she want at this time of day? Wilf had sorted out her problems only last night.

'Coming,' he said.

He opened the door and she bounded in.

Her face was radiating intimacy. Her black hair was like coal.

'Could I borrow some sugar, please!' She held out a cup.

Wilf said, 'Sorry, I'm right out of sugar.'

She looked into his food cupboard. 'And right out of everything else, too.'

Miss Chong took Wilf's hand and led him one floor down to her flat which was tidy and smelled of cooking.

'But ...' was Wilf's attempted protest, but Miss Chong was adamant.

'I will cook you nice meal,' she said.

Miss Chong was in her middle twenties and had a traumatic lovelife and it was for advice that she constantly hounded Wilf. Not that Wilf minded. His television set had not been working for some time and he found that his evenings dragged interminably. He would read books, stolen from the library, for hours in the bath. Not a very pleasant way to spend his evening as he would have to spend some unpleasant time removing splinters of enamel from his person. Wilf was a lonely man and she was a lonely girl. Her father was from Hong Kong and her mother was from Ellesmere Port. Miss Chong was therefore a half-caste. Wilf liked her in an objective sort of way. Wilf was objective about almost everything. Miss Chong had often thought she had offended him for he often ignored her, but Wilf would drift into a world of his own and think of things as they might have been.

'Actually, I'm not really hungry, Miss Chong.'

Wilf looked at her slim body and felt a certain warmth.

'I've told you to call me Sally,' she said, hovering around her tiny fridge.

'All right, Sally,' Wilf agreed. 'At least let me help you.'

'You stay there,' and she pushed Wilf back into his chair.

Silence fell. Then came the sizzling of frying fat.

'Sounds nice,' said Wilf.

Julian and Malcolm watched the female traffic warden walk up to Julian's Rolls.

'Let's invite her in,' said Malcolm.

'With Sambo in pieces,' scoffed Julian.

She looked at Julian's parking permit and passed on.

Julian shrugged.

Sambo's entrails were smeared all over them.

Julian gulped down some cognac, then gulped down some more.

'I'd better be pushing off,' he said. 'I've got some business to attend to.'

Julian sniffed.

He smashed his fist into the palm of his hand.

He kissed Malcolm.

And wearing just a pair of bloodstained underpants, Julian got into his car and drove back to his flat.

Sally Chong gave a broad smile and said, 'Here you are, Wilf.'

Wilf grabbed a magazine and put it on his lap to insulate himself from the steaming heat of his hostess's offering.

Mushrooms, bamboo shoots, bits of egg. It looked, thought Wilf, like so much spew.

Dutifully, he tucked in.

'MMmmmmmmm,' he said. 'This is really tasty.'

She smiled and sat next to him.

He became uncomfortable. 'How's your lovelife?' he asked.

'I have finished with my new boyfriend. He was no good for me,' she answered. 'I took your advice.'

'But,' said Wilf, almost choking, 'I didn't advise you to end your relationship.'

'He only want to feel my loolies,' she explained, and cupped her small breasts as if to demonstrate.

'Some men are like animals,' said Wilf.

'Most men are like animals,' corrected Sally Chong.

Wilf could sense that something was going to develop and he wasn't sure if he wanted it to. Wilf's life had been one long menopause up to now, perhaps it was going to be all right from now on.

He felt her moving closer. A shred of onion wedged itself in his dentures.

She said, 'Would you like some coffee?'

Wilf said that he would.

Sally smiled. She was always smiling.

'I must do some shopping afterwards,' she commented. 'Will you come with me?'

'Aren't you working today, then?' enquired unemployed,

chomping Wilf.

Sally Chong smiled almost inscrutably.

Julian also lived in a top flat although his was more penthousish than atticish.

Three bedrooms, two bathrooms, etc., etc., ...

He arrived there and startled the cleaning woman.

'You're all covered in blood, sir,' she observed.

'I cut myself shaving,' said he.

She scuttled away.

Julian ran some bath water and fed his goldfish and pondered on his morning's work.

He was lounging in the bath, having a Martini, when his phone bleeped.

He said, 'Fuck!' rather vehemently, and reached for it.

There was a beep ... beep ... beep ... beep sound as, somehow, somewhere, in a telephone booth, a coin was pressed into a slot.

A sleazy voice said, ''ello, Julian.'

''tis I.'

'Julian, it's me, Alf Tramp,' the voice went on. 'I'm out ...'

Julian heard a clunk followed by the dialling tone.

Julian heard himself scream slightly.

The phone dropped from Julian's hand. Sheer terror had overcome him. The dreaded Alf Tramp, scourge of the underworld, was out.

Julian gathered what senses he could and stepped from the bath. He took hold of a goldfish and bit off its head.

'Alf Tramp.'

He spat it out.

'Alf fucking Tramp ...'

For the first time in a long time he thought of Wilf. He thought of Wilf's obscure abode. He felt safer already.

Julian got his leather-bound, gold-lettered address book and looked under 'A' for Ant. All that was there was a telephone number.

Julian picked up the phone.

He dialled the number.

After quite a while a young but weary female voice said, 'Hello. Geoffrey Harvey and Company.'

'Could I speak to Mr. Grudge please?' asked Julian impatiently but politely.

'Grudge has been booted ... er, I mean, ... em ... Mr. Grudge don't work here no more.'

Julian could hear muffled whispering.

'Can I have his address, then!' he snapped.

'Hold on,' said the voice.

Julian thought he heard muffled giggling.

Julian sucked the guts from the dead and de-capitated goldfish and shouted 'aaaaaaaAAAAAArrrrrrrrr!!!' because they were most unpalatable.

'Hello,' said the voice.

'Yes,' said Julian, as he swilled down three Valium with goldfish water.

'Are you a client?' asked the voice.

Julian hissed, 'Tell me what I want to know or I'll ram my shoe up your fanny.'

'Promises, promises,' said the voice.

Julian felt frustration and anger and fear.

'I'm fuckin' warnin' you!' he screeched. For he had degenerated into the language of the gutter and this was always a bad sign.

'All right, all right,' the voice relented. 'Got a pencil? Two hundred and forty, Canning Street, Liverpool. Room Twenty. Are you happy now?'

Julian let the phone drop.

He would hide out at the Ant's place until Tramp's re-imprisonment.

But first he would say sorry and goodbye to the woman.

Half an hour later, Julian was dressed in a smart suit and standing outside a smart apartment building. He pressed the number five button. An electronic voice said, 'Who is it?'

'Julian.'

The door buzzed and he pressed it open.

Within seconds, Julian had Deborah in his arms. He kissed her neck and looked at her breasts and put his tongue in her mouth and felt her bottom.

Then Julian noticed a man's comb on the floor. He pushed her away and picked it up.

'To whom does this belong?' he demanded.

She quickly looked away.

Julian opened the first bedroom door. It was empty. Then he opened the second. A fat, middle-aged man lay naked and huddled in the flower patterned sheets.

Julian's hands shaped themselves into claws. His face became a mask of insane rage.

'No, Julian,' begged Debbie.

He cast her aside.

The paunchy little man cowered and whimpered.

Julian took the man's bottom lip into his claw and pulled. It ripped away.

Debbie screamed.

The man screamed.

Julian screamed.

All for different reasons.

Julian took a tight hold on the man's scrotum and pulled. Something snapped.

'God,' said Debbie, and vomited.

Julian punched the man in the gut and said to Deborah, 'I've told you what will happen if you carry on like this.'

'What about you and Malcolm,' she replied. 'How do you think that makes me feel …?'

Her eyes were beginning to wetten.

He kissed her on the cheek.

She wiped some traces of sick from her mouth and kissed him on the end of his nose.

He saw the warmth in her eyes and he was afraid.

'I'm going away for a few days,' he said. 'Alf Tramp is after me.'

'Christ,' she said.

And Julian wondered if she really cared.

Then Debbie said, 'Will you give me one before you go?'

'Just a quick one,' he said. 'Just for you.'

Julian placed seventy pounds beneath the pillow and the paunchy man was kicked to the floor. His groans accompanied the squeaking of the bed.

Wilf carefully steered Sally around an Alsatian turd..

It was the first time Wilf had been out with a woman for years. They were both about the same height, Wilf and Sally, and they made a fine couple. Sally had linked her arm around his and this made Wilf feel quite proud.

They entered a small supermarket and Sally took a wire basket.

'You should hold this,' she explained, handing Wilf the

basket, 'while I choose the food we need.'

Wilf took the basket.

He liked the sound of 'We'. A long time since he had been part of a 'We'.

Sally lifted in some potatoes. Heavy potatoes.

Wilf's interest was aroused by a rack of magazines. Imported American ones. Sally dragged him away. 'None of that,' she grinned, and put a loaf in the basket.

Wilf felt a little guilty, allowing Sally to pay for the goods. But all his money had been given to Smith. He would have to end his association with Smith.

It was unhealthy.

Back at Sally's flat Wilf said, 'I'll go and change.'

Sally said she would start to cook their dinner and that there was a good programme on television.

Wilf felt wanted.

Wilf went up to his room.

He put on his jeans and his sweatshirt and his sandals.

He became "The Bohemian".

'Ooh, Wilf, you look lovely,' said Sally.

Wilf blushed.

Sally sniffed. 'You need bath,' she said.

Wilf blushed again.

Alf Tramp was waiting outside a phone booth.

Alf Tramp was a very big fat man with scars on his face. His hair was short and spiky and his teeth were huge and brown. His face was unshaven and his breath smelled. The prison wardens had sighed with relief at his departure.

Alf Tramp was an amoral gorilla.

An American car screeched up.

'What's wiv de flash mota?' Tramp asked his chauffeur.

'The Boss just nicked it,' answered the besunspectacled, greasy Italian. 'Nice, re-spray, isn't it.'

Tramp grunted in agreement.

Tramp got in beside the Italian and the car screeched away.

'I hear you're out to get Julian, Mr. Tramp,' said the Italian, smiling obsequiously.

Tramp gripped the Italian by his lapels and butted him in the face.

The Italian managed, somehow, not to crash. He felt great

pain. Worriedly, he felt his nose and jaw for' fractures.
'The very sound of his name makes me see red,' said
Tramp.
'Sorry,' said the Italian, wiping blood from his nose.
Tramp stared out of the car window and saw the world.
Tramp felt great anger.

Julian phoned Malcolm and asked him to look after the
Rolls and a few other things. Malcolm was horrified when
he heard about Tramp and fully supported Julian's plan of
escape.
They said, 'Bye bye,' to each other ...
Julian was on the train to Liverpool.
Alone in a first class carriage. He started to bite his nails.
He was feeling insecure.
He smoked some small cigars and drank from a hip flask
and slept a little bit and looked out of the window and read
a couple of novels and eventually arrived at Lime Street
Station.
When Julian finally reached Canning Street it was almost
nine o'clock in the evening.
The crumbling old houses with naked light bulbs shining
through curtainless windows reminded him of his youth. A
youth of seventeen should never have the mind of an adult.
Julian had never felt loved. Wilf had a lot to answer for.
'So this is where the Ant spends his life.'
Julian's white suit had become creased and grubby. He
needed a shower, he needed a drink. He needed Malcolm to
talk to, Malcolm to hold.
The hand-made shoes clicked on the pavement.
Julian strained his eyes at every house, searching for a
number.
A scruffy boy said, 'Well get a load of the dandy.'
A whore said, 'Hello, bigboy.'
Julian's hand tightened around his flick-knife.

Wilf's hand was inside Sally's blouse. He wasn't quite sure
how it got there.
They had just been sitting, watching television.
Sally purred appreciatively and Wilf felt a little frightened.
It had been a good programme.
They had both found it most interesting.

Wilf's hand was going numb.

Sally suddenly swung her head around and offered her small, wet mouth to Wilf.

In the flickering light of the screen, Wilf could see her little eyes, lightly closed, expectant. He puckered his lips and lowered his head.

There was a knock.

Wilf opened his mouth and Sally opened her eyes. 'Who's that?' she said.

'No idea,' said Wilf.

Wilf knew it wouldn't be for him. Nobody called for him. Even Smith never came to the house.

Another knock.

'It's coming from your flat,' said Sally. 'Someone is knocking on your door.'

Sally seemed to be getting jealous. Was it another woman, just as Wilf was coming out of his shell.

Wilf got up. 'I'd better have a look.'

He opened the door and peered up the tatty staircase to where Julian stood majestically.

His heart leaped. 'Julian, my son!' he cried.

Julian managed to summon forth some saliva and sent a small jet of it hurtling to the dusty floor.

'Ant,' he said.

Alf Tramp was feeling bored in a small terraced house in Battersea.

He was playing patience when there came a polite tap on the door of his room.

Tramp grunted and the door opened.

The Italian, clutching a girl, entered.

Tramp sent the cards flying. The table fell over. Tramp reached out a ham-like hand and gripped the Italian around the throat. The Italian was dragged into a collision of heads and fell, concussed, to the floor.

The girl backed away, scared out of her wits, as Tramp made towards her.

'Show me your arse,' he said.

Tramp locked the door. 'Show it me!' he screamed.

The girl turned her back to him and obliged.

He let his trousers fall to the floor. The girl looked and screamed. She had heard of Tramp's strange tastes.

'Bend over that chair,' said Tramp.

Miss Plimsoll had made herself comfortable in her little divan bed in her small flat above the shop. A tray of buttered scones and a glass of milk stood on her bedside cabinet. She was finishing the final chapter of a biography she had borrowed from the library.

A moth hovered above her, crashing into the pink lampshade every ten seconds or so.

She reached for a scone.

Outside, cars were whizzing past and people were talking and laughing.

She bit into the spongy, buttery whiteness.

Her left hand had gone beneath the sheets and had sneaked under her flanellette nightdress and was tickling her 'down there'.

It helped Miss Plimsoll to relax.

Smith lived two streets away from Wilf. Smith, at Wilf's request, had never called upon Wilf.

Smith thought he looked smart in his suit. One could always tell quality. If one bought better class clothes they would last longer. It stood to reason.

Smith could remember his father telling him 'hold your head up high, son. Keep up your standards and there's nobody who will bring you down. Only you can do that.'

They were wise words.

Smith wasn't very good at cleaning pots and pans and things like that. It was woman's work.

Smith felt little compassion for anybody.

He had seen both sides of the coin. He had lived it up with the best of them and dossed down with the worst. But always had he kept up his standards. Never once did his standards drop.

A camera on a stand, some lights, a bed, a sinkful of dirty dishes.

Smith wore a grey tie. Blue badges all over it. Lots of people thought it was some kind of club tie and often expressed interest.

People in pubs asked about it.

Smith had bought it in a jumble sale for ten pee.

He rubbed his eyes and yawned.

All his life he had lived in Liverpool. Liverpool, with its nasal, bronchial, good-hearted folk.

A two-up two-down in Scotland Road, just across the way from Paddy's market. Kids staying off school because they had no shoes. Policemen's boots, some of them used to wear. Frail, rickety legs coming out of huge black boots. The other kids used to mock. Smith's dad never let him mock. If he had mocked those kids Smith would have got a clip across the ear. Smith's dad was a docker, before his bronchitis and arthritis got too bad. The dockers would be in cages and a man would shout 'We'll have you, you, you, and you, and you ...!!' and the rest of the men would go home.

Smith's dad would come home.

'My dad died of despair!' shouted Smith.

Smith had loved his dad. His long suffering dad with his hands covered in segs and his fingernails bitten down with worry. Smith's mum never seemed to feel anything. 'Like water off a duck's back', his dad would say. She would cook whatever she could afford to buy.

She would always put the children before herself.

She would never say very much.

Smith couldn't even remember what her face looked like.

There were things in Smith's life that made him physically wince when he remembered them. Memories that made his spine tingle with a sense of injustice.

Smith was a very sensitive man.

His dad had bought him his first camera from Paddy's market. He had made Smith go for a walk while he bought it so Smith wouldn't see how much it cost.

The money could have bought meat and shoes.

But Smith's dad had wanted Smith to be a photographer.

Smith was a photographer.

Julian and Sally and Wilf sat around the scratched coffee table and stared at one another. Julian was feeling sick, Wilf was experiencing new emotions, and Sally was hurt that Wilf had never told her that he had a son.

'So this is where the Bohemian Ant lives,' said Julian.

'This is it,' said Wilf.

Sally sipped instant coffee silently, not taking her eyes off Julian.

The atmosphere was heavy.

Julian felt at home in the squalor. He knew it was his own level to which he would return one day. The luxury pads, the Rolls, they were all figments of his imagination. The only thing that was tangible in his life was his body. He would feel it at night, just to make sure it was still there. Sometimes he had his doubts. Who needed a Rolls Royce? It had been a mistake. It had all been a mistake. He should never have been born. Wilf had a lot to answer for.

Wilf looked at Julian's suit. It would cost or it would have cost Wilf two month's wages to get a suit like that. Wilf knew of Julian's criminal activities and Wilf knew how stupid he had been not to embark on a life of crime himself.

What hurt Wilf was the fact that Julian had changed his name. He had been christened 'Howard Grudge', but was now known as Julian Jones.

A tear formed in Wilf's eye.

He knew that Julian was ashamed of him. A father should command respect. But why did Julian hate him? Times were hard then. Wilf had tried to do his best.

Wilf, in his mind's eye, saw Howard the schoolboy and was proud.

Wilf saw Julian the man and was proud.

Sally sipped in silence.

Tramp was grunting. The girl felt as though she was being ripped apart. She screamed and she screamed and Tramp grunted all the more. Tramp was used to the pimply flabby bottoms of his sycophantic cell-mates. The bottom of the pretty young girl turned him on considerably.

Tramp came, very profusely, very quickly.

Miss Plimsoll pushed back the sheets and got out of bed and went to the bathroom.

She had kept her teeth this long and didn't intend to lose them now.

Julian said, 'Look, Ant, I'm in a spot of trouble. There's a man after me. I simply must hide.'

Wilf tried to look concerned.

Sally said to Julian, 'Would you like something to eat, Julian?'

Julian said, 'Yes.'

Wilf scratched his head and sent a shower of dandruff onto the table. 'What have you been up to?'

Julian shrugged. 'Nothing to worry about. Just a bloke who's out to get me.'

'I've got a sort of cockloft place above my flat,' suggested Wilf. 'But why don't you use a hotel. You'd be more comfortable.'

'A cockloft sounds fine,' said Julian. 'I need to come to terms with myself.'

The atmosphere was very heavy.

'Have you been maiming people again?' asked Wilf.

Sally slowly rose to prepare some food. She could hardly take her eyes off Julian.

'A few here, a few there, but nothing like the old days.'

Wilf felt uncomfortable as Julian's staring eyes met his.

Wilf said, 'When d'ye think you'll make me a grandfather?' and smiled weakly and gulped.

Tramp asked, 'What's your name, darling?'

The girl, sobbing on the bed, said, 'Bill.'

Tramp grinned. 'That's a boy's name,' he said.

'My dad always wanted a boy. He wanted to call him Bill. He hated me 'cos I wasn't a boy.'

Tramp put his huge arm around her soft white shoulders. 'Bill,' he said endearingly. 'I like that, Bill.'

The girl disengaged herself. 'Can I get dressed now?'

Tramp nodded.

She seemed to have difficulty in walking.

Tramp soaked in the sight of her small firm buttocks, but five orgasms was enough for any creature.

She dressed quickly and went for the door.

Tramp said, 'Aren't you staying the night? I wouldn't mind a cuddle.'

The girl shook her head, unlocked the door, and left.

Tramp lay back on the bed. It was just a small room in a house that the Boss used now and again. It had a bed and a chair and a sink and a gas ring. It had food. Tramp could stay there until he got established again. Tramp's brain began to think. Three years ago, Tramp had received a parcel through the post. Naïvely thinking that somebody had sent him a present, Tramp had eagerly opened it. Tramp and Julian had been colleagues in those days. Tramp had considered Julian his friend. Tramp had been involved in a lot of 'work' with the Boss and had given his son and heir, Batman, a beautiful, blue-eyed, bouncing boy of three, to Julian. Julian hadn't minded looking after Batman. He had been willing. Too willing. Tramp had loved Batman with all his heart.

He had hated to be parted from him. But, Tramp's huge ungainly brain had reasoned, it was only for a week or so. And how Tramp had attacked the pink wrapping paper and purple ribbon. And how childlike the grin on his pockmarked and dirty face had been.

When Tramp had opened the white box, a shrivelled little thing fell out and dropped to the floor. Tramp had picked it up and had screamed and wept and had torn out his hair and had said very rude words.

For the shrivelled little thing in Tramp's neanderthal palm had been Batman's severed penis.

It was the last bit of his son that Tramp would ever see again.

Tramp had gone berserk and had been rash and was consequently jailed.

Tramp cried hot tears and felt agonizing grief.

Tramp felt in his pocket and brought out an empty Alka Seltzer bottle. Empty, that is, except for a quantity of formalin and Batman's preserved, hacked off organ.

Tramp looked at it.

And cried a good deal more. And wondered why Julian had done such a thing.

Tramp gave an angry-animal scream.

There was a sound of scufflling on the floor. The Italian was recovering. Tramp watched him slowly rise to his knees.

Tramp, putting the bottle back in his pocket, said, 'Cook me something to eat.'

'My head ... ooooooooohhh, my head' said the Italian, and went into a peal of his native tongue.

'Talk fuckin' proper, you foreign cunt,' said Tramp, and sent his boot thudding into the wretched fellow's shoulder.

The Italian, clutching his head and rubbing his shoulder, staggered to his feet.

'What would you like, Mr. Tramp?' he asked, in a humble,

long-suffering voice.
'Steak!'
The Italian fumbled around in a food-filled cardboard box.
'Sorry. There is no steak here, I am afraid.'
Tramp roared.
Tramp collapsed.
'All you need,' said the Italian maternally, running his artificially tanned fingers through Tramp's spiky hair, 'Is a good night's rest.'

Deborah drew back her curtains and looked at the London night.
She heard the London traffic.
The fat man was asleep. She envied him.
She hadn't sent any money home for two weeks. Her mother would be worrying about her. For Deborah was a considerate girl. Every week she would put two ten pound notes in an envelope and address it to the little council house in Leeds that had once been her home.
She had moved to London seven years ago when she was sixteen and had found herself a tiny Earls Court bedsit. The gas-ring had leaked and the tap dripped all night but Deborah put up bright pictures of pop singers and burned incense and things weren't too bad.
Then she met Julian.
Julian told her he loved her.
Julian had ponced for her.
Julian had lived off her.
Julian had left her.
She took another sip from the brown ale bottle. She put six sleeping pills into her mouth and washed them down.
She lay down on her bed and looked at the portrait of Julian that was hanging on the wall.
Deborah threw the brown ale bottle, but missed. The bottle did not break.
She wanted to sleep but could not.
Deborah reached beneath the mattress and brought out her vibrator.
She was laughing.

Wilf suddenly remembered that he should have gone to the doctor's. He scratched his bottom.

'Still got the same old trouble?' asked Julian.

It was obvious to Sally that the father-son relationship was a little strained.

Discreetly, she stayed in the background, making cheese sandwiches.

'Too right,' answered Wilf.

They made an odd pair, sitting opposite each other, trying hard to break the ice.

'Is Sally your woman, then?' asked Julian. 'Are you going to marry her? Is she going to be my new Mum?'

Wilf blushed.

Sally grinned.

'I am still married to your mother,' said Wilf. 'And I am always likely to be.'

'You say that as if you don't want to be,' snapped Julian.

'Oh, don't let's argue about it,' Wilf said calmly.

Sally placed a plate, laden with cheese sandwiches, on the table. Julian grabbed eight of them and stuffed as many as he could into his mouth.

'So that's what your posh friends teach you,' quipped Wilf.

Julian spat out masticated pieces of bread, margarine, and cheese. Most of them landed on Wilf.

Wilf jumped up. 'You dirty little ...'

Julian moved fractionally forward in his chair. 'What was that, Ant?'

Wilf sat down and commenced picking the foodstuff off his sweatshirt.

'Eat it,' hissed Julian.

'I'll get some beer,' said Sally, and she left.

When she was out of earshot, Wilf said, 'There's nobody here for you to impress, Howard ...'

Wilf was looking into Julian's eyes. They were beautiful eyes. Wilf felt proud that he was looking into such eyes.

'I have told you before. My name is Julian. My name is not Howard. Do not call me Howard again.' The words were slow and emphatic.

Wilf looked away, the way he always did. Wilf would always back down.

Julian stuffed the rest of the sandwiches into his mouth.

There was a musty smell. Cooking was the dominant odour. But there was an underlying smell.

Wilf stared at his foot.

'How long ago was it that you booted me out into the
street?' Julian munched.

Without looking up, Wilf said, 'Nobody pushed you out of
the nest. You were welcome to stay ...'

'Like fuck,' interrupted Julian. 'You wanted me out. You
gave Mum hell. You were a stinking bastard. Why couldn't
you have made me happy. Why didn't you have a good job
and give me love ...'

Wilf looked at his son. There was pain there. Wilf hadn't
caused his son pain.

Wilf had never hurt anyone. He put his hand out and rested
it on Julian's shoulder.

Julian felt the warmth of the hand seeping through his
jacket.

Wilf said, 'Son ...'

Julian threw the hand off him. 'Don't call me that.'

Wilf said, 'I got the sack today.'

Julian immediately smiled.

'I thought that would please you,' smiled Wilf. 'I told
Harvey he could ...'

'Spare me the pathetic details, you cretinous Ant,' sneered
Julian realizing that he was coming dangerously close to
liking the old man.

'Don't reject me, son,' said Wilf. 'It's silly, after all this
time.'

'There's only one way I'll ever forgive you,' said Julian.

'And what,' asked Wilf, 'is that?'

'I want you to make me a caterpillar suit.'

'A what?' queried Wilf.

'Caterpillar suit. You used to be good with your hands. It
shouldn't present too much of a problem to one so
talented.'

Wilf helped himself to a bit of chewed sandwich.
'Hmmmmm,' he said. 'What do you want a caterpillar suit
for? What is the point?'

'So people will look at me,' explained Julian. 'So I will be
different.'

'That's reasonable,' opined Wilf.

They looked at each other with some understanding now.

'I was also caught shoplifting,' said Wilf.

Julian laughed. 'What did you pinch?'

'Some tights and a few other things.'

'Good man,' said Julian.
'But I got away,' explained Wilf. 'The pigs didn't get me.'
This time it was Julian's hand that went across. Wilf felt its
coldness.

Miss Plimsoll was asleep.

The Italian had given Tramp twelve aspirins and was
busily undressing the brutish man.
Tramp was murmuring, 'Batman ... Batman ...'

Malcolm's hand brushed through Adrian's hair. 'Adrian,
you sonofabitch,' said Malcolm affectionately.
Adrian sighed.
Adrian loved Malcolm but Malcolm loved only Julian. He
felt a great fondness for Adrian but had never slept with
him. Adrian wished he would.
'How long is that roughneck going to be away?'
'Julian is not a roughneck,' defended Malcolm.
'No?' retorted Adrian. 'Then why does he vivisect helpless
nig-nogs?'
'You promised you wouldn't mention that again.'
'All right, I'm sorry. But you know the way I feel for you,'
sobbed Adrian. 'I'm jealous, damn it all. Jealous of the
relationship you and Julian have.'
Malcolm and Adrian held each other tightly.
'You can stay with me tonight,' said Malcolm.

Wilf, Sally, and Julian lay together in Sally's bed. Sally was
in the middle.
They had both insisted that Wilf washed under his armpits.
They had been drinking beer and felt a little drunk. Sally
put a bucket under the bed, just in case.
'No sex please,' said Sally. 'We just cuddle and be friends.'
It was going to be a strange night.
Wilf woke up in the middle of it. Sally had her arms around
him and Julian was muttering. He moved Sally's body
towards Julian's and silently got out of bed.
Through the window shone the strange light of the city.
Just a star or two shone in the sky. It was a cloudy night.
Wilf went to a chair and sat down. He was beginning to
wheeze. He had always had breathing problems. The beer

had given him indigestion. Bottled beer always made him
feel like that.

He burped and said, 'Excuse me.'

Julian was with him. Julian wanted him to make a
caterpillar suit. A man was after Julian.

Julian.

'My son.'

Wilf was indeed getting old.

His forearms were flabby.

He was no longer in control of his body. It did whatever it
wanted to. He had no control.

Growing old. He was becoming senile.

Sally's firm young body had excited him. He had felt her
little breasts through her brassière. Firm young breasts.
Half Chinese breasts.

Julian would make love to her, Wilf was sure of this.

Good luck to him.

Julian had a firm body.

He had work-outs in gyms and played tennis and squash
and his stomach muscles were like steel.

Julian was tough.

Wilf would get back into bed and cuddle Julian. His
paternal love. His heart.

'Julian, Julian, my only son ...'

A half-chewed cheese sandwich remained on the plate and
Wilf picked it up.

'Julian, my son ...'

Wilf's voice had always been high-pitched. At school they
used to say he had no balls.

Wilf had always been mocked.

Phoebe had used him. Taken advantage of him.

People had said that Julian was not his. That he had been
duped, taken for a ride ...

But Julian was his. Phoebe had said he was. 'This baby's
yours all right,' she had said. 'What are you goin' to do
abart it?'

Wilf smiled.

And nibbled at the sandwich.

He took a deep breath, held it, then exhaled.

The wheeze persisted.

Living was indeed hard.

Wilf was now unemployed and he owed rent. He also owed

money to Smith.

Wilf's mind felt tired.

Julian had done well for himself. He knew how to make money.

Julian had been in prison.

Julian had a criminal record.

Wilf crept to the bottom of the bed and took Julian's wallet from the discarded white jacket.

Wilf wheezed and coughed.

Sally had a pretty nightdress on that showed the gentle curves of her body. Sally was a nice person. It had been her idea to sleep three in a bed. Sally was a lonely person.

Julian was muttering still, and grinding his teeth together. Was he dreaming about the man who was out to get him?

Wilf opened the wallet.

Money.

Crisp banknotes.

Wilf counted them.

Ninety pounds.

Wilf took four five pound notes and put them in his pyjama pocket. He had bought the pyjamas four months ago and they had never been washed. Wilf hated clean things.

Harvey had once asked him to put a clean shirt on. Bloody impertinence.

'Harvey can go and screw himself,' said Wilf.

He put the wallet back.

Tiredness was crawling over him but he had to stay awake. He had to make Julian the caterpillar suit. Then things would be all right between them once more.

Wilf needed Julian's love.

Wilf wished he'd seen the doctor.

He scratched and cursed. And wheezed.

Julian let out a particularly disturbing cry.

Wilf felt the banknotes.

Harvey could stick his job.

Miss Plimsoll woke up.

'Blast,' she said. 'Blast, blast, blast.'

It was unusual for Miss Plimsoll to feel so strongly about anything but this was the fourth time in four nights she had been woken up.

She put her empty milk glass to the wall and applied her ear.

She heard heavy panting and the squeaking of a bed.
It was the couple who lived in the flat above the wine merchants.
Miss Plimsoll tried to listen to the words they were saying.
She heard: 'darling' and 'mmmmm' and 'that's nice' and 'faster, faster, don't stop' and quite a lot of other little snippets.
Miss Plimsoll had had enough.
She put the glass back on her cabinet.
She clenched her fist and went 'Bang ... bang ... bang' on the wall.
The noise stopped immediately.
Miss Plimsoll smiled.
Miss Plimsoll. Miss Evelyn Plimsoll. Her friends called her Evie. Long hot summers spent at the tennis club. Flies buzzing in the afternoon sun. Long walks through the country. Riding horses. Long skirts. Church on Sunday and helping Mummy to shell the peas.
Miss Plimsoll slept.

Tramp was sprawled over the bed. The Italian had quit the scene. Tramp grunted and shifted position.
Tramp was in No Man's Land.
Tramp, against his conscious will, farted loudly and wetly.
Tramp shifted position.
Julian had murdered Batman. Julian had eaten Batman. Lovely little Batman.
Tears seeped from beneath Tramp's closed eyelids.
Tramp had eaten Batman's mother. Her name was Nancy. She had a fine body and Alf Tramp loved her once. They lived in South London and were happy. Alf was a forklift truck driver and Nancy worked in a cinema, selling ice-cream. Then Alf got friendly with the Boss. It was an impulsive thing, eating Nancy. He didn't eat her all up, of course. He just hacked off a bit of leg and roasted it as if it were lamb. The Boss had sold the rest to a restaurant. Nobody missed her. Funny how nobody misses anybody like her.
Tramp knew he was ugly.
He knew he was ugly and bad-tempered.
He wished he hadn't hurt the Italian.
The Boss said he should have an operation on his brain. Said he needed help.

Alan Brown

The Boss was always right.

The Boss never seemed to go to prison.

Tramp puzzled about this.

Tramp always seemed to be in prison. He met Julian in prison. Julian had been a good person at first. Julian had been nice to him at first. And Tramp had been nice to Julian.

Julian had been a good friend.

Why?

Why had he sent Batman's little willy through the post like that?

Tramp was in love with Julian.

He wanted to kiss him and hold him.

Tramp had told Julian about eating Nancy.

It had amused Julian.

Tramp scratched his leg.

Nancy had loved him.

He used to drive his forklift truck very fast and try and knock people over but it was all in good fun. It used to go 'wwwwwwwwiiiiiiiiiizzzzzzz' and skim along. On Fridays he would get a brown envelope and take it home, unopened, to Nancy, and she'd kiss him and open it and put some money in the "Baby Jar" and she would say, 'only another four months and we'll be able to afford to start a little Baby Tramp.' Alf would kiss Nancy and she would serve him egg and chips and they would go for a walk and hold hands and listen to the radio.

She had been a good wife.

Alf had eaten part of her leg.

He would go out to the pub and Nancy and the Boss would sit at home, watching the television the boss had stolen for them.

Nancy said they just talked.

Julian said the Boss was no good.

The Boss gave Tramp money.

The Boss was the Boss.

The Boss had given Tramp a watch. It said 'To Tramp from the Boss,' on the back.

The Boss was a funny little man with a funny little moustache and he sold second hand cars on wasteland.

Julian had beautiful eyes and lots of money.

Tramp didn't have anything much. Tramp felt for his

bottle.
Tramp shifted position.

Smith never went to sleep before five o'clock. He would lie awake and stare in to nothingness and wonder about profound things. Smith was not a happy man.
Smith was lying in his bed in the basement room in which he lived and worked.
In a good week he could earn two hundred pounds. In a bad week he could earn nothing.
Smith was not a good photographer.
His prints were grainy and blotchy.
But people bought his work.
Little men like Wilf who never had the real thing.
Wilf would spend seven or eight pounds a week. Wilf owed Smith money.
Smith was younger than Wilf but looked older. Smith had been in the war. Smith had fought for his country. Wilf hadn't.
Smith looked at his latest batch of pictures.
The hard face of a Liverpool scrubber, complete with scar and broken teeth, looked back at him.
Christine was a good poser.
Her husband didn't mind her working for Smith.
Christine didn't mind pushing beer bottles into her vagina.
Christine's husband was unemployed and they needed the money.
Smith had seen every part of Christine's body. He had taken photographs of every part.
Smith looked at his watch. It had stopped at half-past two.
Sometimes, when Smith looked up and out of his window, he would see the legs of people.
Smith had seen many knickerless women in his time.
No longer was Smith turned on by the sight of a fanny, be it covered in hair or bald. Smith was totally immune to sexual excitement. Penes did nothing for Smith either.
Only money motivated Smith. Smith was a capitalist. He had four thousand pounds, almost, in the bank. Not bad for someone without formal qualifications.
Smith had never loved.
Smith put down the photographs and thought he could hear rain.

Wilf had taken some dresses from a cupboard. One was green, one was pink, one was red. He had slashed them into strips and was now sowing them together in a fashion which, Wilf thought, best resembled a caterpillar.

Wilf.

Wilfred Howard Grudge, unemployed.

Harvey would be lying in bed with his wife. Feeling her body as she slept. Dirty Harvey who looked up the typists' skirts. Catching a glimpse of Valerie's bum.

A blister formed on Wilf's second finger, where the scissors had rubbed.

Wilf pricked it with the needle and sucked out the watery stuff.

Wilf hadn't seen a caterpillar for ages.

He had seen one in Sefton Park once.

Wilf used to go to Sefton Park quite a lot.

When the weekends came alone and the sun started to shine he would buy a loaf and a piece of cheese and some tomatoes and make some sandwiches and go to the park.

Little children would play.

Grown-ups walked their dogs.

And Wilf would lie on the grass and try to get burned by the sun.

The last time he went, some little girls had asked him if he was mentally ill and jokingly he said he was and the little girls ran away and told their friends and they all came back and congregated around Wilf and Wilf blushed and grown-ups started to look at him as though he was some kind of molester and Wilf didn't go again.

Julian was still muttering.

A voice said, 'What are you doing?'

Wilf jumped.

Sally stood in front of him.

'Making a caterpillar suit.'

'With my dresses,' scolded Sally.

'I thought they were old ones,' said Wilf.

Sally asked, 'Do you want something to drink?'

Wilf gave a wheeze. 'No thanks.'

He held his chest.

Sally knelt beside him.

Wilf knew she was after a poke.

Julian muttered.

Sally looked at Wilf and said, 'Come back to bed. You're not well. You can finish it in the morning. Julian won't mind.'

'I want to put it by the side of his bed so he sees it when he wakes up. I used to do that at Christmas time. He used to try and stay awake all night but he never quite made it. He used to come into our bedroom and kiss me and Phoebe ...'

Sally kissed him on the forehead. 'You are a good man. But you be ill if stay up all night.'

'I want to finish it. He expects it of me.'

Sally got up and started to make some coffee.

Wilf continued sewing.

Wilf didn't know if he wanted to have sexual intercourse with Sally or not. It seemed a bit of a waste of time. Wasting valuable sewing time.

Wilf always threw the pictures he got from Smith away after a couple of days. A waste of money.

Wilf had twenty pounds.

He would pay fifteen pounds off his rent arrears and give five to Smith.

He would tell Smith to get stuffed.

It was pathetic.

Julian wouldn't like it.

Wilf was worried about the way Julian cried out.

Why didn't he cry out "Daddy!"?

Sally Chong was wearing her little nightdress. Sally Chong was making a cup of coffee and thinking about her parents.

Wilf rubbed his eyes.

Sally was back beside him.

'Wilf,' she said, and put her hand on his leg.

Wilf stiffened.

The kettle started to boil.

Smith turned off his light and settled down for sleep. He would stay in bed till eleven. That was when the new girl was coming round. The girls came to him. He asked them to strip and he examined their bodies. He turned a lot of them away. There were so many ugly bodies around.

A lot of men would like to have Smith's life.

But Smith was a very unhappy man.

Miss Plimsoll was dreaming peacefully of her teaching

times.
' … Please, Miss. Johnny's peed his pants.'
Evie got up from her desk and went to investigate.
Little Johnny had urinated over all and sundry.
Evie led little Johnny into the staff toilet and took his
trousers down.
Little Johnny looked around him.
Evie took hold of little Johnny's tiny penis …
Miss Plimsoll smiled in her sleep.

Tramp had fallen out of bed.
He rubbed his leg.
Alf Tramp had a reasonable physique.
He had used the prison gym a good deal. In prison, they
had taught him how to read and write.
They didn't like Tramp in the prison.
He knew that he wasn't very popular and that people were
scared of him. Julian was scared of him.
He had bitten Julian in the mouth once.
Julian had called him an ox.
Tramp got back into bed and scratched his bottom. There
was a spot on it.

Malcolm and Adrian had consummated their relationship.
Adrian was very proud of himself and Malcolm felt deeply
ashamed.
The hacked body of Sambo, lying in the bath, had
something to do with it, one can be assured. Adrian was not
above blackmail.
Malcolm knew that he would have to tell Julian.
Julian would kill him.
Malcolm and Adrian were in bed together. Malcolm was
smoking a cigarette.
He didn't often smoke.
Malcolm hated Adrian.
'How are you going to dispose of the body?' asked Adrian
coldly.
'Oh, shut up,' said Malcolm.
'I have a suggestion to make,' said Adrian smugly.
Malcolm ignored him for a suitable amount of time.
Then he asked, 'What is it?'
Adrian removed the cigarette from Malcolm's fingers and

dropped it into the ashtray.

He pressed his lips to Malcolm's ear.

Malcolm squirmed.

'Tell you in a minute,' whispered Adrian.

Julian was being chased by Tramp. Tramp had a big knife in his hand and was shouting. 'Give me back my Batman! Give me back my Batman!'

Julian woke up.

He had the bed to himself and there were voices coming from the living room.

He ached all over.

He needed a drink.

He wished Malcolm were with him.

Julian was sick and tired of everything. He should take less valium, travel more.

But even his trip to San Francisco hadn't refreshed his zest for living.

Julian's soul was dying.

Malcolm understood him. Not many people got close enough to do that.

In the bad old days he had been happier.

What had he let himself in for?

What was happening?

He considered getting up and going to the toilet. He would see what was going on in the next room.

But it was too much of an effort, getting out of the cosiness of the bed.

Tomorrow night he would sleep in the attic. Things were becoming unreal. Had to get a grip. Steal some babies. Their meat was the tenderest.

He hadn't meant to eat Batman.

Perhaps Tramp would understand that.

Hadn't even meant to kill him.

But the little devil had been making a hell of a lot of noise.

And when Batman was dead, Julian had been curious as to the taste of the flesh.

He did send Tramp a momento ...

Julian went back to sleep.

Sally's smooth fingers started to sooth away Wilf's self-doubts. The caterpillar suit was finished.

'Come back to bed,' whispered Sally. 'Julian is well away.'

She led Wilf.
Wilf followed.

The Italian woke Tramp with a smile and a cup of tea.
'Here you are, Mr. Tramp,' he said.
Tramp rubbed his eyes and yawned.
'Ta,' said Tramp.

Julian awoke and saw his caterpillar suit.
'Yipppeeeeeee!!' he enthused.
This woke Wilf and Sally.
'You like it, son?' asked red-eyed Wilf.
'It's lovely.'
Julian leaped out of bed and tried it on. It was a little long
in the leg but apart from that it fitted perfectly.
'I'm glad you like it,' said Wilf.
Sally kissed Wilf on the cheek and went to make some
breakfast.
'I'm a caterpillar,' sang Julian, 'I'm a caterpillar ...'

Miss Plimsoll had been awake for some time. She had
breakfasted on a hard-boiled egg and three toasted slices of
brown wheatgerm bread.
She liked her flat above the shop. It was all she needed.
In another half hour she would go down and open the door.

Smith slept.
He was dreaming about money.

Malcolm and Adrian had exhausted themselves.
They were too tired to dream.
A strange smell pervaded ... Sambo's body had started to
decompose.

The Italian drove Tramp, the Boss, Billy the Boot, and
Knuckles to Julian's flat. Tramp pushed the cleaning lady
to the floor when she opened the door.
Knuckles and B.B. fondled their machine guns lovingly.
'Where's Julian,' spat Tramp.
The cleaning lady shook with fear.
'Better answer the man, lady,' said Knuckles, taking a
bottle of acid from his pocket.

'Mr. Jones's flat is number six. Right at the top,' said the cleaning lady.

The Boss had been following Julian for some time. He stared enviously at the Corniche that glistened in the morning sun.

'Any of you guys fancy a lay?' asked Tramp, kicking the cleaning lady.

The Boss slowly shook his head.

B.B. said, 'No thanks, I just had one.'

'She's too old,' said Knuckles.

The Italian said, 'I do,' and looked at the Boss for approval.

The Boss gave a wave of his hand and the Italian dragged the middle-aged woman into a cupboard beneath the stairs.

Tramp smashed his foot through Julian's front door.

The flat was empty.

Tramp gave a scream and commenced destruction. Knuckles and B.B. joined in.

Half an hour later the Oldsmobile drew up outside Malcolm's house.

Adrian and Malcolm were still asleep, locked in each other's arms.

Tramp leaned against the door and it burst open. They all poured in. It was Knuckles who found the two homosexuals. He let out a 'Yahoooo!' and the others came running.

Tramp grabbed Malcolm by the hair and said, 'Where's Julian?'

Malcolm gasped and Adrian shook.

B.B. took hold of Adrian by one of his nipples and dragged him out of bed.

The Boss said to the Italian, 'Put the kettle on. I'm parched.'

Tramp butted Malcolm in the mouth.

The Italian reluctantly went to make a cup of tea for his employer.

Knuckles went over to help his colleague torture Adrian.

Tramp started to take his trousers down.

Adrian screamed as a droplet of concentrated hydrochloric acid landed on his prepuce.

The Boss said, 'Quiet boys, I've got a splitting headache.'

'Sorry, Boss,' said B.B. and he hacked Adrian's tongue out with a razor blade.

Tramp plunged into Malcolm who had started to cry.

The Italian came back clutching Sambo's severed head and said, 'Look what I've found.'

Sambo's glazed eyes stared at them.

The Boss said, 'Where's my fucking tea?'

Julian felt nice and safe inside his caterpillar suit. He had decided that a caterpillar made a high-pitched mating call like this: 'mmeeeemeemeemememmmmmeee.'

Sally led Julian with a length of string and Wilf led Sally by the hand. People stared at the trio as it progressed along the Liverpool streets.

'Mmmeeeeeeeeeeeeeeeeem.'

Julian hopped and leaped and walked normally as well. He wished he could lie on his tummy and crawl like a caterpillar but Sally said there was too much dog muck on the sidewalk and he would get himself dirty.

The trio entered Boots, the chemist.

'Mmeeemeeeeeeeemmmeeeeeeee.'

Julian got down on his knees and went round and round in circles.

Sally shouted, 'Help. A caterpillar. Somebody help me!'

A crowd of salesgirls and customers formed a circle around them.

'Meeeeemmeeeeemmmmmmmeeeeeeeee.'

Wilf took out his plastic shopping bag and scooped ointments, pills, sunglasses, anything he laid his hands on, into it.

'Meeeeeeeemmmmmmmmmeeeeeeeeeeemmee.'

'Help. A giant caterpillar.'

Wilf filled the bag and left the store.

The manager had arrived.

Sally said, 'It's my husband, sir. He thinks he's a caterpillar. What can I do?'

The manager adjusted his spectacles.

Julian stood up. 'I'm frightfully sorry about this,' he said. 'But these things come over me every once in a while. I used to be a civil servant, don't y'know.'

The manager pulled at his right ear.

'Would you mind awfully, sir,' said Sally, 'if we just left and took a taxi home?'

Julian sobbed, 'I'm a failure. I'm a failure.'

Sally comforted him.

The manager said to one of his staff, 'Mary, call a taxi will you.'

'Thank you, sir,' said Sally.

Smith woke up. Somebody was tapping on his window.

He looked at his watch.

He jumped out of bed and put on his dressing gown.

One room wasn't big enough for him any longer. He would have to get a bigger place. Something more middle class.

He pulled back the curtains and stared into the face of a new would-be model.

He opened the door and said, 'Come in.'

She sniffed as she entered.

Smith said, 'Take your coat off. Sit down.'

He watched as the young woman removed her coat and headscarf. She had long black hair and a clear complexion. Her nose was too big and her cheekbones too pronounced. Her yellow shift dress touched her knees and hung like a sack.

Her flat red shoes were scuffed and unpolished. A slight bulge of her abdomen heralded the arrival of another mouth to feed.

'What's your name, love?' asked Smith.

'Denise. Christine said it would be all right for me to come.'

Smith got the impression that her sinuses were made of sandpaper.

'That's all right, Denise,' he said. He held out his hand and said kindly. 'My name is Mr. Smith.'

Her hand was limp and cold. Smith squeezed it reassuringly.

'Sit down,' Smith said once more. 'Make yourself at home. I haven't had my breakfast yet. Ho ho ho.'

'Do you want me to come back later?' asked Denise.

Smith took some mouthfuls of whiskey.

Denise looked at him stupidly.

'No, no. Whip them off. Let's have a look at you.'

She looked at the window. 'Don't you think I'd better close the curtains.'

Smith looked her straight in the eye. 'Look, do you want a job as a model or not?'

Denise nodded and said, 'Would you unzip me please?'

She turned her back to him and he obliged.
He watched her strip to the skin.
'Come here,' he said.
She walked towards him.
He cupped her breasts with his small hairy hands and said,
'Mmmmmm. Quite firm.'
Then he said, 'Open your legs,' and he ran his fingers
through the hairiness and murmured 'Mmmmm. Quite
soft.' Then he felt her buttocks.
He asked her to lie on the bed with her feet in the air.
He asked her to kneel on the bed with her bum in the air.
He asked her to do a lot of things.
In the end he said, 'I'm sorry, love. Come back and see me
when you've had junior.'
There was sadness in her eyes.
He swilled some more whiskey.
She said, 'I don't suppose I could do anything for you …?'
Smith said, 'I never mix business with pleasure.'

Miss Plimsoll took a chocolate bar from the display and
unwrapped it. Things had been very slack so far. All she had
taken was a pound.
Miss Plimsoll munched at the chocolate bar and stared at
the wall where the pictures of ice-lollies added to the gaiety
of the decor.
Her sister had invited her down to Penzance for a long
weekend but there was nobody to look after the shop.
Miss Plimsoll munched and thought.

Knuckles showed the Boss the piece of paper he had found
in Julian's flat.
The Boss looked at it closely.
It read: 'The dirty stinking Bohemian Ant – 051 236 4563.'
'Some kind of code, perhaps,' said the Boss.
Tramp took a look at it and passed it on to the Italian.
'It is telephone number,' said the Italian.
Malcolm said, 'I will tell you nothing, you swine.'
Knuckles wanted to chop Malcolm's throat but Tramp
said, 'No, I like him.'
Adrian was unconscious on the floor. Blood was oozing out
of his mouth.
The Boss gave the piece of paper to Billy the Boot and told

him to make enquiries. B.B. went into the hallway.
'I'll tell you nothing,' said Malcolm.

Sally and Julian got into the taxi and it drove away. The manager waved sympathetically.
Sally said, 'To Canning Street, please.'
At the traffic lights, the driver stopped.
From outside came a tap on the glass. The driver jumped when he saw the apparition on the other side of the window.
'It's all right,' said Sally, as Wilf clamboured inside. 'He's a friend.'
'Mmmeeeeeeeeeeeeeeeeeeeee.'

Billy the Boot had verbal intercourse with Harvey's switchboard operator. He was told all about Grudgey Groo's dismissal and gathered that Ant was Julian's father as Wilf had often boasted to the staff about his hyper-successful son.
B.B. was given Ant's address.

Wilf patted the plastic bag. 'Not bad for a morning's haul, eh?'
Sally smiled and searched for her door key.
Julian asked, 'How was I?'
'Just great, son,' said Wilf. 'Just great.'
A light breeze was carrying dust particles into eyes, nostrils, into lungs.
House sparrows chirped and searched for food amongst the debris that littered the sidewalks. A man in a black suit and open-necked shirt had stopped an old lady and asked her for a light for his cigarette.
And Wilf watched the taxi until it disappeared round a corner. Then he followed the others into the house.

Knuckles asked, 'What are we going to do with him, boss?' nodding in Adrian's direction.
Somebody said, 'We can't take him to Liverpool with us.'
Adrian was beginning to come round.
His penis was on fire and his mouth felt as though it were filled with molten lead.
He wanted to say, 'Kill me, just kill me, for God's sake,' but

it just came out as an imbecilic gurgle.

The Boss ran his fingers through his moustache and thought.

Sambo's head had been kicked under the bed, out of sight.

Knuckles, Billy the Boot, Tramp, the Boss, the Italian, and Malcolm all stared at Adrian and thought.

Suddenly Malcolm said, 'Why don't you get some more acid and give him an acid bath?'

Tramp looked at Malcolm proudly as if to say 'that's my boy'.

Knuckles clapped his hands together gleefully.

'Then,' continued Malcolm, 'we can get rid of Sambo at the same time.'

They all nodded with approval and the Boss instructed the Italian to get some more acid and they all had another cup of tea.

Miss Plimsoll was fed up. Why should she have to work in a silly shop when the sun was shining outside. She would go out and catch some sun.

Mr. Jenkins, who had been calling for years for his tin of 'Guano Flake', arrived at the door of the shop just as she was shutting it.

'Sorry,' said Miss Plimsoll. 'I'm closing.'

'But,' protested Mr. Jenkins. 'I must have my "Guano Flake". This is the only shop in the whole of London that sells it.'

'I'm sorry,' said Miss Plimsoll, shutting the door firmly, 'but the shop is closing for the day.'

'I'll die without my "Guano Flake" ...'

Miss Plimsoll didn't approve much of smoking. It was bad for the health and the wallet. One day, Mr. Jenkins would thank her.

Wilf, Sally, and Julian sat around Sally's coffee table and looked at the product of their endeavours.

'May I share it out?' asked Julian.

'Sure, son,' said Wilf.

'One for you, one for you, one for me,' said caterpillar Julian. 'One for you, one for you ...'

Sally took hold of Wilf's hand and guided it to her thigh.

'I love you,' she whispered.

Smith picked up his suit from where it lay next to the full chamber pot. His nostrils were filled with the smell of strong ammonia.

A sudden attack of housepride compelled him to pick up the receptacle and carry it to the sink where he poured the contents over a stack of dirty dishes.

'With ammonia plus,' he couldn't resist saying.

He took another mouthful of whiskey and picked dirt from between his toes.

Miss Plimsoll hadn't had her bathing costume on for some time and she thought she had better try it on to see if it still fitted her.

She stared at herself in the full length mirror. It was a little daring but Miss Plimsoll was in a naughty sort of mood.

Yes. It would do admirably.

She took it off. Her breasts were still quite firm for her age, but Miss Plimsoll had never had any children.

Poor Evie. It was too late. Her chance had come and gone.

'I will never be a mother,' she said to herself.

Her voice was full of sadness.

But it wouldn't do. Life must go on. The lido waited.

'Nil desperandum, Plimsoll.'

She caught a glimpse of her reflected pudenda and saw black stubble emerging.

Miss Plimsoll made a mental note to buy some more razor blades.

The Italian staggered back into the mews house carrying a huge bottle.

'Not in here, stupid,' rebuked the Boss, as the Italian made his way into the living room. 'Take it into the bathroom.'

They all followed the Italian, leaving Adrian to gurgle on the floor, and watched as the immigrant poured the fluid over Sambo's remnants.

'Go and get the head,' said the Boss to B.B.

'Go and get the head,' said B.B. to Malcolm.

Malcolm went back into the bedroom and started to search beneath the bed.

Adrian got to his feet and tried to attack him.

Malcolm had always had a desire to maim somebody with his bare hands but propriety had always stood in his way.

But now things were different.

'Gurgle gurgle gurgle,' said Adrian as he took a swing at Malcolm.

Malcolm ducked and said, 'Ah so,' and gave Adrian a rabbit punch in the kidney.

Then Malcolm kneed Adrian in the testicles and pressed his old friend's arm so far up his back that it broke.

Malcolm smiled.

Adrian was in a heap on the floor, moaning, groaning, and gurgling.

Malcolm raised his heel and was about to smash it down on Adrian's head when B.B. stopped him.

'Don't do that, mate,' said Billy. 'We want him to be wide awake for his bubble bath.'

'Sorry,' apologized Malcolm. 'I forgot.'

Billy waited as Malcolm sought out the head and together they went back to the bathroom.

Things were fizzing along nicely.

'Don't half fucking pong,' said Tramp.

Malcolm dropped the head in.

Sploosh!

Julian had put his white suit back on, set fire to his caterpillar suit, and was feeling bored.

Wilf said, 'Look son, why don't you go down to the corner shop and get some sweets or something.'

'I should really be preparing the attic for my vigil,' replied Julian.

Sally's flesh was melting beneath Wilf's fingers.

Sally was in love with Wilf.

Darling Wilf.

Awareness came to Julian.

'You dirty Ant!' he cried. 'You want me out of the way so you can have your way with yellow fever. You smelly little Bohemian.'

Ant became afraid.

Sally became tense, anxious.

'You're kicking me in the balls again, aren't you?' continued Julian. 'Just when I was ready to forgive and forget.'

Sally took the initiative and put her arm around Wilf's offspring.

'There, there, my little caterpillar,' she said in a soft voice.
'Wilf loves you. I love you. Don't get angry.'
Julian brought out his flicknife and opened it. The blade
scintillated.
'Put it away,' said Sally.
Wilf gulped.
'Not until I've dealt with the Ant.'

Smith had cut himself shaving but the blood on his face had
almost dried. Sitting, wearing his suit, on the edge of his
bed, he had been working hard.
A pile of letters enclosing postal orders, cheques, and
banknotes had been sorted out. The customers who had
sent cash and postal orders could have their photographs
by return of post. The others would have to wait. Smith
could not be too careful.
All he had to do now was to sort through his *Money Owing*
book.
Wilf's name was at the top of the list.
Smith would have to visit Wilfred Grudge.

Evie Plimsoll felt happier than she had felt for a long, long
time. She walked with a skip and a bounce. She felt alive.
Under her arm she carried a rolled towel in which was
rolled her bathing costume.
She was thinking, 'I'm going to the lido, I'm going to the
lido,' the way her children used to sing in the playground.
The words were different, of course, but the same
enthusiasm was there.
She would go to Penzance. She would shut up the shop.
She would sell the shop and buy a little cottage in the Isle of
Man. All her relatives had advised her against buying the
shop. It had been silly, buying the shop.
Miss Plimsoll had never before felt so irresponsible.
She found that she was looking at men's faces. Staring at
them. Looking at the tops of their legs for a tell-tale bulge.
Evie had never seen a grown man's penis. She had seen
little boys' penes and she imagined that a man's was just
the same as a boy's only bigger and perhaps with a little
coarse hair growing around it.
Evie had wanted to be a nun.
Her sisters had laughed at her. They had all wanted to

marry into good families and lead lives of luxury.

And one night, Evelyn had woken up. She had the little boxroom all to herself because it was only big enough for one bed. All the other little Plimsoll girls were fast asleep in the other bedrooms. Little Evie, with her long pig-tails and purity, saw an angel. The angel smiled. An angel with long golden hair and dressed all in white glowing beautifully by the window. Evie had closed her eyes. She wasn't scared or frightened. When she re-opened her eyes the angel had gone.

She had never told anybody about her angel. To tell would be to cheapen the whole thing. And besides, they wouldn't have believed her.

Evie's angel never came back.

Evie had waited all her life in vain for the angel to return.

Evie's angel.

Billy the Boot and Knuckles held Adrian down while Malcolm tied Adrian's hands and legs behind his back, the way they tied steers in rodeo shows.

Malcolm made sure the knots were tight and that the coarse rope hurt Adrian's tender skin.

Adrian knew of his fate and struggled.

He still wanted to express the sentiment that if they had to kill him they could at least do it in a humane fashion.

'Gurgle, gurgle, gurgle ...'

The Boss said, 'I think we're going to need some more acid.' He threw the car keys to the Italian.

The Italian was a funny sort of chap. He had come to England, ten years ago, with his parents. His mother made pasta and his father served customers in a restaurant in Soho. And working for Joe Harper wasn't too bad. He was always giving Mario the dirty jobs but Mario didn't mind. Anything, Mario reasoned, was better than working in a restaurant.

'Well get a move on, then,' said the Boss, raising his voice a little.

The Italian left.

'Gurgle, gurgle, gurgle ...'

Miss Plimsoll bumped into a man on the stairs going down into the Underground.

'Sorry,' said the man, and he touched her shoulder.
The man went but a tingle, in her whole body, remained.
Someone had touched her.
A man had touched her.

Joe Harper looked at his men. Billy the Boot, Knuckles, the Italian. What a shower they were. Wastrels, derelicts, human filth. Joe Harper had given them a modicum of respectability. At least they were employed. At least they were getting regular incomes. It was all because of his efforts. He had got together a small amount of money and rented the allotment. Second hand cars, stolen cars, rusty old bangers. People wanted cars and Joe sold them cars. Robbing sub-post-offices came later. Coshing rent collectors – every little helped. Now he was selling newer cars to better people. Joe had done well for himself. He would offer Tramp a partnership one day. Tramp had been Joe's whipping boy for too long.
Joe knew he was a grubby, small-time hood.
He knew he was unsophisticated, inarticulate, shabby, and greasy.
He wanted to change all that.
Joe needed Julian.
Joe wanted to learn from Julian.
How to cheat, how to be fraudulent, how to appear respectable. Joe wanted to learn all this and more. Joe wanted to make it into the big time. Pull off a few bank robberies, bribe policemen, blackmail government officials, knock over wages vans.
Joe was getting old and he would have to do something quickly.
The Italian, Knuckles, Billy the Boot. All of them yobs.
Tramp was just as bad.
Deriving pleasure from watching the suffering of others. It was awful.
But Joe would let them have their fun. Joe was good to his workers.
After all, Malcolm looked like a good fraud merchant and Malcolm was very loyal and Joe liked that. Perhaps Malcolm would get Joe and Julian together.
Joe and Julian Enterprises.
Joe rubbed his hands together with glee.

He would talk Tramp out of killing Julian. Joe knew that Tramp fancied Julian.

The Boss sighed.

What a queer set-up it was. Eating human flesh. Acid baths. Not Joe's cup of tea.

Joe thought of the times he had copulated with Tramp's wife and he thought of his own good wife and the son he had at a very good school and he thought of Julian and he smiled.

A quarter of a million in the bank, substantial share interests, couple of houses abroad, a few nice cars, a good pair of shoes ... the Boss's ambition was quite simple. He just wanted money, status, power, and respectability.

Wilf said, 'Go on then, kill me. Slash my flesh and spill my blood. Do you really think I care anymore?'

'Don't say such things,' said Sally.

'Keep out of this, yellow-peril,' hissed Julian.

Wilf closed his eyes and at any moment honestly expected that he would feel the presence of cold steel in his body.

Julian's hand was going sweaty. He stared at Wilf and then looked at the knife.

The knife dropped to the floor.

Wilf opened his eyes and breathed. 'Whew ...'

Sally breathed a sigh of relief.

'The Ant will live another day,' smiled Julian.

'Do you still have to prove to me that you're a hardcase, son?' asked Wilf sympathetically. 'We all know you are. We all know you're a helluva guy ...'

Julian started to blush and lowered his head in embarrassment.

'Let's all go and get some sweets,' suggested Sally.

They all smiled and felt happy.

Miss Plimsoll stepped into the Tube train and sat down next to a coloured gentleman, just to let him know that she wasn't prejudiced. Miss Plimsoll believed that we were all different coloured flowers in a big beautiful garden. It had been a long time since Miss Plimsoll had travelled beneath the ground. She never usually went outside a radius of a quarter of a mile from the shop. Why should she? She had everything she needed within her little circle.

Her head jogged as the train zoomed along.

The man sitting opposite her was looking up her skirt.

Miss Plimsoll didn't look anything like her age. She had often been mistaken for a woman of forty or forty-five. Her face was unlined and her body was trim.

Miss Plimsoll always sat with her legs apart. It had always seemed right and proper to do so.

She knew the man was looking up her skirt.

The thought of it gave her pleasure.

She even parted her legs fractionally wider.

He was a middle-aged man dressed in a trendy manner. He clutched a briefcase to his chest as if it contained priceless gems.

Miss Plimsoll tried to catch sight of his bulge but couldn't.

The coloured gentleman got up. It was Miss Plimsoll's stop, too. She got up and gave the peeping man another quick flash.

Miss Plimsoll heard the chatter of Americans, Spaniards, Germans, as she walked to the ticket barrier.

She handed her ticket to another beautiful flower.

Up the stairs and she was free.

Miss Plimsoll sucked in the air that swam all around her. Free as a bird. Free as a fish ...

Hyde Park was just across the road. She made towards it.

'Screeeeeeech!'

She jumped.

A nasty looking man shouted, 'Watch where you're goin', you silly fuckin' bitch!'

Miss Plimsoll didn't know where to look.

But it had been a very nice car with the steering wheel on the wrong side. It had shone very brightly.

The trees were blowing gently. Pigeons were at her feet.

Miss Plimsoll held her breath and ran very quickly across the road. She had always had good lungs and she still did her breathing exercises regularly.

Miss Plimsoll would live to be a hundred. She would get a telegram from the Queen. If only she had some grandchildren and great grandchildren to show it to.

Smith was really bored.

He sat on the hard wooden bench at the bottom of Leece Street and tried to read his paper.

It was no good.

Opposite was the dole building. The Department of Health and Social Security. A place that Smith knew well. Smith bought his own insurance stamps for Smith was self-employed. But not all that long ago, Smith had gone there every week to collect money to keep alive.

He had read a sentence five times already.

Smith. A shabby man sitting on a wooden bench trying to read a paper.

Sometimes he would go to the library and get himself some books. Sometimes he would get books about photography and sometimes he would get novels. He would go back to his room and climb into bed and cuddle a pillow and read out aloud and his throat would get sore and he would drink some whiskey. After four chapters he would be drunk and carefree. And then, perhaps, if a model came round, he would take some photographs. Sometimes he would get out his big mirror and take self-portraits. Smith had many self-portraits.

It was a good enough life. He was his own boss.

Smith had a brother in Canada who kept inviting him over for a few months but Smith had always refused. He was a little frightened of going in an aeroplane.

'Come on, you can afford it,' said the letters. Smith could afford it. The change would do him good.

'Damn,' said Smith.

He had just remembered that the public health inspector was calling.

'Damn.'

Cheeky sod. Last time he had called he said Smith's place had bugs.

'Cheeky sod.'

Bloody nutter he was. Had a little hat on and wore bicycle clips to stop the bugs going up his trouser legs. Said 'Ssssshhhhh' to Smith and suddenly pulled back the mattress. Smith hadn't seen any little black things scuttle away. And the wallpaper was all right too. How could anything live behind wallpaper?

'Bloody nutter.'

You could report them if you liked and get them the sack. They were public servants. If they got cocky and superior you could report them and they would lose their jobs.

Smith had read all about it in a book.

Smith smiled.

The public health inspector could knock and knock and knock but he would get no answer.

Smith would be out.

The Italian returned with more acid and Malcolm surprised himself by saying 'About time, you sleazy rattlesnake.'

'Sleazy rattlesnake!' bellowed Tramp. 'I like that. Sleazy rattlesnake ...' Tramp laughed.

Even the Boss said, 'Sleazy rattlesnake, heh heh ...'

'Sleazy rattlesnake,' said Knuckles and Billy the Boot in unison. 'Ha, ha, ha ... sleazy little rattlesnake ... ha ha ...'

The Italian went hot all over and placed the cannister on the living room floor.

'Not there!' shouted the Boss, 'In the bathroom.'

Tramp, in an attempt to impress Malcolm, kicked Mario in the head as he bent down to lift the acid.

The poor Italian screamed with pain.

'Sleazy rattlesnake,' giggled Tramp, and he looked at Malcolm for approval.

Malcolm giggled and said, 'You are strong, Tramp.'

The Italian lay groaning on the floor.

'Wanna go?' invited Tramp.

And Malcolm, not wishing to offend Tramp, said, 'Okay', and kicked the immigrant in the bottom.

Tramp chuckled.

'All right, joke over,' said the Boss to the Italian. 'Get up.'

And he indicated for Knuckles and Billy the Boot to help their pain-wracked colleague take the acid into the bathroom.

Adrian had been watching with terror in his eyes. Time was running out for him.

An acid bath, for Christ's sake. An acid bath ...

Hadn't he been a good boy?

Hadn't he always washed his hands after going to the toilet?

Hadn't he always managed to fart silently?

Hadn't he done his best to solve the ecological problem?

And now this.

They had hacked out his tongue and burned his private part. They had tied him up. They were going to plunge him into a gurgling, stinking bath of acid ... Malcolm would suffer for his treachery. They all would. They would suffer.

'You know, I could use a boy like you,' said the Boss. 'Can you drive?'

Malcolm had a brand new Lotus outside and had gone rallying when he was at Oxford. And this cretinous criminal was asking him if he could drive ...

'Yes,' said Malcolm.

'I think I may be able to fit you into my organization. I want to move into the fraud game, you see,' explained the Boss, 'and I need people with brains. What do you say?'

'What do I say?' said Malcolm, with great enthusiasm. 'What do I say? I'd be a real hood. Could I wear a black shirt with a white tie?'

'Sure you can,' drawled the Boss.

Tramp said, 'You're in,' and fondled Malcolm's buttocks.

'Of course,' the Boss drawled on, 'You'll have to start at the bottom to begin with. Till you get the hang of things. Dig?'

'Sure,' said Malcolm.

The Boss smiled.

'We're ready in here!' shouted Knuckles.

Tramp picked up Adrian and carried him towards the bathroom.

'Mind if I take some movies?' asked Malcolm.

'Sure,' said the Boss. 'But call me Boss. I like people to call me Boss.'

'Yes, Boss,' said Malcolm. 'Thanks, Boss.'

Tramp held Adrian over the bath and the others stood back. Malcolm shouted 'Action!'

Adrian's eyes were closed. He could smell the acid. He could hear it. He had seen Sambo's remnants at the bottom of the tub. Soon he would be like that. Any second ...

Tramp giggled sadistically.

'Action!' repeated Malcolm.

Tramp giggled.

Adrian prayed.

'Drop the fucker!' shouted the Boss.

Adrian plunged downwards and screamed. Acid splashed over Tramp and he screamed.

The Boss grinned.

'It's burning me, it's burning me,' Tramp moaned and danced.

Adrian was gurgling horribly and trying to get out but couldn't.

Things went quiet.

Adrian died.

Malcolm stopped the camera and said, 'Shit! I forgot about the lights.'

'Never mind, there'll be plenty more,' consoled Joe Harper.

'Sure, Boss,' said Malcolm.

Deborah woke up.

Julian used to have a nickname for her. He called her Sperm-whale.

Her face tightened into a sort of smile.

She supposed it had something to do with sperm.

For Deborah did seem to have had more than her fair share of sperm. Gallons of different kinds of sperm had been pumped into her. Fat men, thin men, tall men, short men. All rich men. Deborah would never look at a poor man. Why should she?

Her head ached.

She had taken, she thought, too many sleeping pills.

She looked over the edge of the bed and saw the spread-eagled corpulence of the sleeping fatman.

A director of a big company. A responsibility to thousands of men and their families. A wife and children and au pair at home.

Her spit landed on his face.

Deborah closed her eyes for a moment.

Then she opened them and looked at the man again and suddenly had a feeling that he was dead. She felt his face and it was cold. Then she got a mirror and pressed it against his lips.

The mirror was unmarked.

Deborah got dressed and, without washing, went to the building society where she kept all her savings. She withdrew everything. Then she went to the post office and bought a stamped envelope which she addressed to her mother. Deborah put the money inside the envelope, sealed it, and posted it.

Miss Plimsoll was surrounded by nature. How happy she was. She felt as though she were twenty again. She would sell that silly shop and buy herself a cottage in the Isle of Man. Perhaps she would meet a nice young man who would want to come and live with her.

Miss Plimsoll thought she looked very pretty in her swimming costume. There was not a pinch of surplus fat on her anywhere and that was because she looked after her figure. She did exercises every day so she would keep trim and beautiful, because Miss Plimsoll did believe she was beautiful. Why else did all those men look at her lustfully? They wanted to ravish her and take advantage of her. That was the way men thought.

The sun re-appeared from behind the clouds and Evelyn Plimsoll once more felt its beneficial warmth.

What had she done with her life? What had she got to show for her three score years and eight?

Miss Plimsoll, who had never felt the joy of having a penis inside her vagina, lay in the sun in the lido in Hyde Park and wished.

Julian had picked up a letter, addressed to Wilf, from the hallway floor.

Wilf and Sally were holding hands and wondering what it could be.

'Shall I open it and put you out of your misery, Ant?' asked Julian jovially.

'Yes, all right,' said Wilf.

Sally squeezed Wilf's hand.

Julian tore open the envelope and took out a crumpled, jam-stained piece of paper.

'*Dear Shitface*,' he read, '*I want some money from you. If you don't send it you'll be sorry you dirty shite-rag and I'll tell everybody what a shit you is and you can't even shag a woman proper not like my Herbert so send it care of the post office in Dublin and make it enough for me and Herbert to go to Australia to start a new life and send it quick or you'll be sorry and send it to Mrs. Phoebe Grimes.*'

'Is that all there is?' asked Wilf.

'It would appear so,' said Julian.

'What a funny letter,' said Sally.

'Who's it from, Ant?' asked Julian.

'Presumably from your mother,' answered Wilf.

Julian ripped the letter into tiny pieces and threw it on the floor. 'What a horror she must really be,' he said. 'Poor Ant'.

Wilf was secretly glad Julian felt this way. 'I'd better get some money from somewhere,' he said sadly. 'After all, she was my wife.'

Sally put her arms around him and said, 'My darling Wilf.'

Julian watched them for a moment. Then he said, 'I'll find my own way into the attic. But remember, if any men come looking for me, I'm not here.'

'Righto, son,' said Wilf.

Julian climbed the rickety wooden ladder. When he reached the dark dustiness he heaved himself up.

Julian was balanced across the small cockloft entrance and was attempting to pull up the ladder which he had found lying on the stairs. Julian's white suit was creased and dirty and his shoes were scuffed. Julian was going to hide in a cockloft that was above Wilf's seedy room in a semi-slum in Liverpool.

Julian felt insecure again.

Smith, for a long time, had been under the impression that some kind of important event was imminent. That something was going to happen.

God, how time dragged.

Smith liked to have something to look forward to. When he was a kid he used to look forward to Saturdays when he would go to the pictures with his Dad.

All through the week the thought of going to the pictures excited and uplifted him. Smith's Dad used to say, 'The secret of a happy life is to always have a goal that you never quite reach'. Smith and his Dad never enjoyed the films they saw but that never stopped Smith looking forward to them.

Smith changed position on the bench. It was really uncomfortable. Smith could stay there as long as he liked. He was a free man and a ratepayer.

Smith had slept on benches.

Smith had done many things.

He yawned, folded his paper, made sure nobody had stolen his wallet, and got up.

He would go and look at movie cameras in Bold Street. Plenty of money to be made in the film world. He would be a film director and make epics and save the British film industry from ruin. The Queen would attend his premières.

Smith would be worthy of his father's name.

Deborah had walked to the bottom of Oxford Street. Shops full of clothes for her to look at. Clothes that she would wear to enhance her beauty.

She felt dizzy.

Her feet were leading her down into Marble Arch Tube Station. It was a journey she had thought of making many times before.

Down the escalator she went, her head spinning.

When she heard the rumbling coming closer and closer she moved to the edge of the platform, closed her eyes, and jumped.

Wilf had just finished kissing Sally when there came a scraping noise from above.

'It is only Julian making himself comfortable,' ensured Sally, and she pressed her mouth against his.

Wilf had never felt a girl's tongue inside his mouth before and he was a little disgusted when Sally did it. Also, he was scared that his dentures would come out and that Sally would swallow them.

Sally wished Wilf would take out his false teeth but was too shy to ask. It was like kissing the inside of a tea cup.

Wilf was not responding very well to Sally's endearments.

'What's the matter, darling?' she asked him.

'I'm worried about Julian,' replied Wilf. 'What are those men after him for? What has my son been doing?'

'It's all right,' soothed Sally. 'Come on, we'll go to bed and I cuddle you to sleep.'

The prospect made Wilf feel better and he unbuttoned his trousers. Sally helped him.

'Just cuddling,' pleaded Wilf.

'Just cuddling,' she confirmed.

They quickly stripped and climbed into Wilf's bed.

It was comfortable enough but really only meant for one. Wilf turned on his side and Sally snuggled up beside him.

'Your feet are cold,' she said.

He moved them away from her in a jerky, clumsy manner.

'What's the matter with you?' she asked, a little baffled.

Wilf grunted.

Through his half-closed eyes, the room looked less squalid,

less unfriendly. A room that many a starving waif would relish. A room that would be paradise to a mental defective. It would keep out the winter wind.

Yes, Wilfred Howard Grudge was lucky in a number of respects. He had a woman for a start. A woman who said she loved him and that was one of the best things a man could ask for.

Wilf pressed his feet back towards Sally's warm body.

'Hhhhmmmmmmmmm,' she said, sensually.

Through one ear, Wilf could hear far-away sounds of motor cars and children's voices.

How could he, with his varicose veins and dandruff and piles attract such a girl?

It was very mysterious.

Wilf was a silly, pathetic, pseudo-bohemian ant and there was no denying the fact. He had married the wrong woman, forsaken his share of the family fortune, and wasted the best years of his life.

He had spent the majority of his pittance on dirty pictures purhcased from the dubious Smith.

He had spawned a son who was round the bend.

Wilf was a gentle person.

Wilf.

He lay in Sally's arms like a small child. Her arms around him felt maternal, soothing.

And Wilf's useless and unproductive life seemed suddenly to pour all over him like a bucket of ice-cold water.

Unemployed.

He closed his eyes tightly and felt himself shiver.

Harvey, in all his professionalism, had fired Wilf. Wilf, who had done his work and said little and who had walked home through the snow of winter and the hazy dustiness of summer.

S-a-c-k-e-d.

Soon he would get his cards.

What kind of nightmare was it to be out of a job. One might as well die. What was life without money.

Wilf said, 'The only pleasure I get from life is escaping from it.'

Sally murmured.

Her comforting arms around him. How many arms in the world could give such joy? Was it a matter of all arms being equal? Was there, somewhere in Honolulu, a pair of arms that could give such pleasure?

Wilf wanted to scratch his piles but thought the gesture would shatter the serenity of the situation.

But wasn't he free? No longer forced to wear grubby suits.

Why couldn't he be young again and be natural and gay and full of love?

Why hadn't he found one single thing in his life that he could give himself to completely. Something he could immerse himself in and forget about all else.

Dreadful melancholy.

Wilf felt Sally's soft lips against the nape of his neck. Her warm breath, her moist tongue, the gentle brushing of her nose. Her fingers massaged their way through the pastures of his lower abdomen.

Wilf, who had stayed up most of the night before making a caterpillar suit, felt his sexual mechanisms creak into action.

'Mmmmmmmmmmmm,' came the warmth at his neck.

Wilf took the opportunity to check his anal aggravation, seemingly without detection.

She had always been the one who had never pulled the chain.

Sometimes there would be a bit of *Daily Mirror* down there too.

Sometimes a piece of cardboard tubing which baffled Wilf.

'Turn round, darling,' requested Sally.

Wilf turned around and faced his bedmate.

'Do you love me?' she asked.

'Of course I do,' he said.

The Boss ordered, 'Go and get a sack!' and the Italian obliged.

Knuckles and Billy the Boot and the Boss and Malcolm looked at one another waiting for someone to say something.

Only the sound of Tramp fishing out bones from the bath could be heard.

The Boss looked out of the window, with obvious pride, at his black Oldsmobile with the dent in the front wing where he had knocked down that long-haired faggot in Hampstead.

Malcolm suddenly remembered he should have been at the opera last night.

Knuckles and Billy the Boot, their minds empty, stared into each other's eyes with a kind of resignation. Knuckles looked down and Billy the Boot shrugged.

Not many people knew that Knuckles and Billy were brothers although their similarity was abundantly clear.

They had little intelligence and even less money, but they did have large muscles and a great sense of loyalty to the Boss. The Boss, after all, did clothe them, feed them, find them women, and paid their widowed mother's rent for her.

Sometimes the Boss called them orang-utans and Knuckles and Billy the Boot took this to be complimentary. Even when the Boss had pinched Knuckles's right bollock very hard indeed there had been no disloyalty.

Billy the Boot and Knuckles could remember the days when they wore donkey jackets and smoked cheap cigarettes and watched television on a tiny screen every night until the National Anthem came on. They could remember their Mum's struggle to bring them up.

They had given their old Mum a colour television for her birthday and she was very pleased with it.

The Boss sometimes loaned them a car so they could drive Mum down to the coast, sometimes Brighton, sometimes Bournemouth.

The Boss liked Mum and even called her "Mum" as though he were one of the family.

Mum was fond of Mr. Harper.

Billy the Boot and Knuckles had a healthy respect for Tramp though they knew, if it came to the crunch, they could handle him ...

Billy the Boot's eyes met Malcolm's and Malcolm felt the bliss of challenge.

The Boss said, 'Put the kettle on, Malcolm, there's a good lad.'

'Yes, Boss.'

Malcolm went into his ultra-modern kitchen. Malcolm knew he lived well.

The Boss did not ask Knuckles or Billy the Boot to make the tea because they wouldn't know where anything was. Anyway, Malcolm was good at making tea. He liked making tea.

'Earl Grey or Darjeeling?' asked Malcolm.

'No thanks,' said the Boss.

Malcolm looked at his hands and felt the dull ache between his legs.

The kettle started to warm.

Malcolm did not really exist.

Nobody was more aware of the fact than Malcolm.

Julian knew exactly who he was, what he wanted, and how to get it.

Julian, in the darkness, felt pity for the Ant. But pity was unspeakable.

Better hate than pity.

Julian knew of the jungle.

Malcolm had said that Freud had said that love was the normal person's psychosis.

To Julian, this seemed to justify everything.

Malcolm used to read many things to Julian. Julian remembered being especially impressed by Nietzsche.

Julian belched and cursed Chinese food.

Then he clenched his fist. He held his breath and punched the space directly above his head. It gave slightly and there was the sound of something scraping and sliding.

Then came the smash as tiles hit the pavement many feet below.

Julian smiled.

He then brought out his flick-knife and hacked away at the roofing felt.

In came light.

Illuminating the dust and the cistern and Julian's once white suit.

It was a good cockloft. Julian's new domain. It was a fine place to be and Julian was grateful.

'My little window on the World,' he said.

And he saw dark clouds above and heard murmuring below.

Batman's meat had been bitter beneath the sweetness, like pheasant. The tiny body hanging upside down, a metal hook through the feet, blood trickling from the throat.

Julian had seen Tramp disembowel a man barehanded.

The stare of the eyes, the spinal shiver, the exodus of excrement, the final exhalation. Julian thought of his own death and he sat on the floor and tried to cry.

He rubbed dirt across his face and thought of cars and backgammon and Malcolm.

For Malcolm's life had been too easy and Julian resented this.

But Julian's struggle had made him tough and sane.

And Julian had struggled. Far harder than the Ant could ever know.

For one night, Friday night, when the Ant was getting drunk, Phoebe told the adolescent Howard that his real father was Bill Henshaw who drove lorries the length and breadth of the country and could fuck women till they drowned in their own come.

Julian took off his shoes.

'Tramp will tear me limb from limb,' whispered Julian to himself.

And Julian lay down and rested his head.

He knew that, when the night came, he would feel the cold.

The Italian returned with the sack and was told to put the bones and teeth of Sambo and Adrian into it.

The Italian had a grandmother who had a painting of the Virgin that cried blood. People would come from all around to look at it.

The Italian felt homesick.

'Hurry up,' the Boss said.

The Italian dropped the last couple of bones into the sack and slung it over his shoulder.

'What are we going to do with them, Boss?' asked Knuckles.

The Boss thought hard.

Tramp thought hard.

The Boss said to Malcolm, 'Come on, you're the one with the brains.'

Malcolm rubbed his cheek.

'Dump them in a pond,' he said decisively.

The Boss smiled proudly.

Tramp winked at Malcolm encouragingly.

'Right,' the Boss snapped at the Italian, 'take the bones to the car.'

'I must put my new tweed suit on,' said Malcolm. 'It isn't exactly right but it will do until I get my gangster gear.'

'Sure,' said the boss.

Smith looked into the window of a coffee bar. Clerks and others were stuffing their faces with plastic eggs and cardboard bread and chemical coffee.
Smith was considering hiring a clerk.
He would entice the creep away from his safe job with a spectacular ad. *'Dynamic young film company requires administrator/clerk. Excellent prospects and salary.'* The creep would take out hire purchase agreements, get a mortgage, run up his overdraft, and then WHAM, Smith would fire him.
Smith instinctively hated office workers. He supposed it had something to do with his Dad.
The thought of it all made Smith's groin flutter.
'Heh, heh, heh,' he sniggered diabolically, and he moved to a camera shop and stared into it.
He knew each camera, each price, by heart.
His eyes took everything in greedily. They soaked up the basic box cameras, they absorbed the sophisticated cines.
He stood there like a statue.
Smith felt in need of a drink.
He strode into the centre of the city, pushing small women and children out of his way.
Smith was feeling successful.
He had just fantasized about his ninth epic and the critics were wild with praise.
'A triumph' the *Echo* had said.
Smith stood outside Central Station and saw the flower seller he had photographed so many times. She saw Smith.
Smith had seen her all over.
'Mr Smith!' she called, her nipples pushing through her tee-shirt. 'Need any more modellin' doin'?'
Smith looked away. He was tired of hangers-on.
'Mr. Smith!'
Smith rubbed his sweating crotch and, taking huge strides, crossed the road.
He saw barrow boys, their faces full of character. He would make a documentary about them.
He would photograph Prince Philip.
Smith would be famous throughout the world.

Wilf's body slid into Sally's.

Sally sighed.

It seemed to Wilf that he had been there before, many years ago, when birds sang happily and the air was filled with the scent of flowers.

'Oh, Wilf,' said Sally.

Wilf looked down and saw the old man lying on top of the young girl. He saw the flabby buttocks rise and fall.

He was disgusted.

But Sally squeezed the way she had learned to squeeze from her glossy magazine.

And faraway, Wilf grunted with pleasure.

Julian removed a piece of old cobweb from his trousers.

He could have Tramp slaughtered any time. But this was all a good game, an amusing game. Julian enjoyed playing games.

Julian giggled.

He pushed his arm through the hole in the roof and stretched out his fingers.

Then he withdrew it and looked at his golden rings.

A long way from Bill Henshaw, Howard Grudge. From Julian Jones.

Julian brought out his small pocket mirror and stared into his own eyes.

Another person looked back with frightening intelligence.

The face gave a nightmarish grin.

Julian giggled and sweated and dropped the mirror and it broke.

Julian, buying *escargots* **when he really wanted fish and** chips. Julian, knowing that people only liked him for the money he spent. Julian, driving his lonely Rolls and not being able to cry.

He took a swig from his hip-flask, put a small cigar in his mouth, and emptied his bladder into the cistern.

Steam rose.

Wilf was going soft.

Sally squeezed but it was no good.

Wilf said, 'I really must go to the doctor's tonight.'

Sally became conscious of his weight on her delicate body and she wriggled in an attempt to find a more comfortable lump in the mattress.

'You see,' confided Wilf, 'I have piles.'

Sally could smell the odour of Wilf's armpits.

'You see how disgusting you really find me,' he muttered quietly. 'I am little more than a derelict. My self-respect has gone completely.'

Sally gave him a hug. 'Silly. You just worried about Julian. I run you nice hot bath and you be clean for doctor.'

'I've got a funny feeling Smith will be round tonight,' mused Wilf. 'I've told him never to call but I've got this funny feeling ...'

Another noise came from above.

They both looked up.

'My son, my son ...' mouthed Wilf.

Wilf plopped out of Sally and she crawled from beneath him.

'He must be cold up there,' Wilf said.

Sally got dressed and went to run the water for Wilf. Wilf was left alone, lying on a bed that was not his, wrapped in blankets that were not his.

Wilf thought of the man who was pursuing his son so ruthlessly. An evil hoodlum, no doubt. A pock-marked villain.

Wilf had heard terrible things about London and what wicked things went on there.

Wilf had only been there once. On a coach. All the others were in couples. Wilf had been on his own. He had seen the advertisement saying 'COME AND SEE THE SIGHTS OF LONDON FOR FIVE POUNDS' and Wilf's summer holidays were drawing near so he went into the little shop and ordered one ticket and the man had asked, 'Just one?' as though it was a crime to go anywhere on your own and a week later the coach left and it took ages to get there and Wilf just looked out of the window at all the cars that were overtaking them and he stayed in the coach when all the others went to the toilet and got cups of tea and they arrived and it started to rain and the driver spoke to them through a loudspeaker and they passed St. Paul's and the Tower of London and Wilf wanted to go to sleep and was glad when they got back to Liverpool and it was very late and he walked back to his room because the last bus had gone and he stayed in bed all the next day ...

You only had to read the papers.
Perverts.
Abortion.
Rape.
Wilf heard the sound of running water.
The bath with the enamel flaking away and the water heater that gave off the smell of burning rubber.
What had happened to the once noble Wilfred Howard Grudge?
Once there had been a beautiful bathroom with carpets on the floor and fishes on the tiles.
Once there had been four meals a day with meat in every one.
Once upon a time there had been potential.
Not any more.
Piles.
Dandruff.
A body that called out for protein.
A woman who pitied, not loved him.
A son who hated him for being the failure he was.
A horde of creditors.
Unemployment.
Loneliness.
What was left?
What was worth having?
Sally shouted, 'It's ready!'
Julian scuffled around above.
Wilf said, 'I don't want a bath. I don't want anything. Have you got any aspirins?'
There were hundreds of aspirins. Wilf had stolen them himself. Enough aspirins to do himself in twenty times over.
It was not real.
He would ring the Samaritans.
The shame of it.
It was too much.

Miss Plimsoll turned on her tummy.
'Blast,' she said.
The sun had been going in and out for ages. And now the wind was getting up.
Miss Plimsoll seemed to be the only person left in the lido.
Everyone had gone except her. She was all alone again.

She wished she had brought her knitting with her.

She was getting cold and bored and a little hungry and she hadn't even been in the water.

Miss Plimsoll decided to give herself another hour and then she would go back to the shop. A nice cup of tea. Toast and a piece of cheese. She could curl up in bed and finish her novel.

Miss Plimsöll wriggled her toes with excitement.

Julian jumped.

'Howard! Howard!' came the noise again. 'It's me, your dad. Let down the ladder.'

The squeaky voice was Ant's. Julian carefully stepped back to the spot where the hinged door was firmly closed. He opened it and let the ladder down.

Wheezing Wilf clambered up.

'What do you want?'

'I was frightened, son. I had awful thoughts.'

Julian could smell Wilf. Wilf, in his dirty, scruffy clothes. The Bohemian.

'Frightened. What has a Bohemian like you to be frightened about. That giant caterpillars might eat you?'

'Don't sneer at me, son,' begged Wilf.

Julian took Wilf by the neck of his sweat shirt and shook him. 'Don't call me "Howard" and don't call me "son". My name is not Howard and I am not your son.'

Then Julian released him, suddenly realizing what he had said.

Wilf looked confused. 'Not my son,' said a faltering voice. 'Not my son. What do you mean?'

Julian lowered his head. 'I'm Bill Henshaw's son,' he whispered slowly.

There was a pain in Wilf's heart. He couldn't breathe …

Julian watched the man in front of him fall to the cockloft floor. He fell heavily, clumsily.

Julian kneeled beside the sprawled figure and looked into the face. The eyes were closed, the mouth was half open. Some of the long greying hair had fallen down across it.

Julian just looked.

Tramp watched as Malcolm locked and secured Julian's

Rolls Royce. Then Tramp watched as Malcolm locked his Lotus. Tramp liked the Lotus and rubbed his groin with approval.

'Glad you like it,' said Malcolm, proudly wearing his new suit for the first time.

The Italian put the sack in the boot of the Oldsmobile.

'She's a real beauty, Boss,' said Malcolm enthusiastically, as he scanned the decade-old American monstrosity. 'I really adore big vulgar cars.'

The Boss grinned smugly.

'Will we get a chance to use our machine guns, Boss?' asked Knuckles.

The Boss looked up at Malcolm. 'You see what I have to put up with? "Will we get a chance to use our machine guns, Boss?" 'he mimicked. 'Tell them, will you.'

Malcolm felt a tingle of pride.

'The Boss thinks, perhaps,' Malcolm tactfully explained, 'that machine gun fire could prove to be a little conspicuous.'

Knuckles and Billy the Boot took this to mean "no" and Knuckles said, 'Okay, Boss.'

Malcolm chose to think that Knuckles was speaking to him.

'You need to pay a visit before we go?' the Boss asked Tramp.

'No, Boss,' said Tramp.

'Right, then,' said the Boss. 'We'd better push off.'

The Boss, Tramp, and the Italian got in the front of the sedan; Malcolm and Knuckles and Billy the Boot in the back.

The Italian started the massive engine, looked in his mirror, indicated, and sedately pulled away from the kerb.

'Why can't you drive this thing,' spat the Boss, 'so that the tyres squeal?'

The Italian gave an exaggerated swallow.

The Boss shook his head with despair and looked at Malcolm again. Malcolm smiled politely and looked out of the window. He watched his beautiful home get smaller and smaller and wondered if he would ever see it again.

Then Malcolm straightened his lapels and stretched his neck, the way all hoodlums did. The Boss took out a cigar. 'Smoke,' he said, and thrust it at Malcolm.

'No thanks,' said Malcolm, immediately wishing he'd accepted it.

The Boss did not smoke it himself but replaced it in his top pocket.

The big, old Oldsmobile moved awkwardly through the London traffic and noisily passed through the gates of Hyde Park.

Tramp, staring directly ahead, his skull leaning forward and resting on the dashboard, broke his silence with a gruff, 'We're here, Boss.'

'Ten out of ten,' quipped the Boss, a little sarcastically, and looked to Malcolm for approval.

Tramp also looked at Malcolm, presumably, Malcolm thought, for some show of loyalty.

Malcolm looked away from them both and felt uneasy. He wished he were with his parents in Switzerland. They were awful bores but one could at least have an intelligent conversation with them. One was at least guaranteed some safety.

Malcolm, a little nervously, started to whistle 'Bonnie and Clyde'.

The Boss joined in.

Then Knuckles and Billy the Boot joined in.

Tramp watched the Serpentine boating lake come into view and the Italian parked the car carefully beneath a willow tree.

Smith banged his fist upon the counter. A smiling young man appeared.

'Hello, Mr. Smith,' said the bank clerk in a friendly fashion, for Smith was respected and well-known in the bank.

Smith picked his nose and scratched his bottom simultaneously. 'Mornin',' he growled.

The bank was empty of customers except for Smith.

Then Smith realized it was afternoon and not morning and he coloured slightly.

The bank clerk smiled again and tickled the end of his nose and Smith snarled, 'Can you tell me how my account stands?'

'Certainly, Mr. Smith,' chirped the bank clerk. 'Excuse me one moment,' and he disappeared behind glass panelling.

Smith, feeling great malice for the neat but rather spotty adolescent, grabbed handfuls of leaflets from the counter and thrust them into his pockets. He also managed to pull a ballpoint pen from its chain.

The bank clerk returned and handed Smith a folded piece of paper.

'Here you are,' said the bank clerk.

'Ta,' said Smith.

And Smith paid in some cheques, gave the clerk a small but adequate tip, and strode out of the bank.

Smith would go home and read the leaflets and have a few drinks. He need no longer fear the public health inspector.

Smith would have a little snooze and then go and see Grudge.

The weather was starting to get chilly so Smith fastened his jacket buttons. He was conscious of a whiskery growth around his chin. The winter was drawing near so he decided to grow a beard. It would help him to keep warm.

Smith. Striding up Bold Street like a man with a mission. Past all the photography shops.

He needed more developing fluid but that could wait. Canada would do him good.

Lots of photographs to be taken there. New horizons. But it would cost so much.

Was it really worth it?

Smith used to spend all his holidays in the countryside. The countryside where they had built the sprawling housing complexes. There had been crystal clear streams and pheasants suddenly flying up as Smith had trekked through the fields. Long free holidays, enjoyable and free.

Now there were people instead of trees.

Smith felt suddenly depressed.

He stopped. He opened his clenched fist and then opened the crumpled piece of paper that was within. Smith saw his bank balance and smiled a happy sad smile.

Smith strode off again but all was not well. Something was wrong with his foot.

Smith looked down and cursed.

The sole of his left shoe was hanging off.

Sally waited at the bottom of the ladder as Julian struggled down with a limp but heavy Wilf over his shoulder.

'Be careful,' Sally pleaded earnestly. 'Be careful ...'

Julian reached the bottom, panting.

'What happen? What matter with Wilf?'

Julian gulped in air and, ignoring Sally, transported Wilf into his room and gently laid him on the bed.

'What matter with Wilf?' she insisted.

'I think,' panted Julian, 'he's had a heart attack.'

'Get doctor,' said Sally. 'I get doctor ...'

She made for the door but Julian grabbed her. 'I think he may be dead already,' he said.

Sally let out a little shriek and held her hand to her mouth. Tears started to form in her eyes.

'Hey,' said Julian. 'Don't cry.'

Wilf was on his bed, looking corpse-like and a little scary. Sally caught sight of him and made a choking sound followed by long, heart-rending sobs.

'Wilf,' she choked. 'Wilf ...'

Julian guided her to the foot of the bed, as there was nowhere else to sit, and moving Wilf's left leg, pressed Sally gently downward.

Julian said, 'I'll put the kettle on and make you a cup of tea.'

There was no reaction from Sally.

'You know,' went on Julian, 'in Ireland they have parties when someone dies. They celebrate.'

Sally had leaned back and was embracing the motionless figure.

Julian watched the panful of water slowly bubble and boil. The Bohemian did not even have a proper kettle. All the years that had gone by and Ant really thought that he had a son. Poor Ant didn't have a son and never would have.

The Ant was dead. At least Julian thought he was dead.

The rhythmic sobbing of Sally and the gurgling of the water. Ant didn't even have a kettle. Ant had nothing.

Julian turned off the gas and walked slowly towards Sally. She looked up at him through bloodshot, bleary eyes.

He sat down beside her and put his arms around her. Then he pressed his face to hers and kissed her.

Sally struggled and said, 'No ... no ...'

Julian tasted the saltiness of her tears. He pressed his tongue into her mouth and laid his hand on her thigh.

'No. Please ... don't,' sobbed Sally.

His hand glided to her crotch.

Through the softness of her pants, he rubbed the coarseness beneath. He stifled her with kisses and she could not speak.

Another hand found her breast and massaged it firmly but considerately.

The fingers moved slowly under the elastic. Sally's whole body stiffened. Julian's palm cupped the small, hairy, moistening fissure.

The fingers worked mechanically.

Sally's eyes closed and she floated a little.

The Julian gave her a small peck on the cheek and removed his hands.

He moved Wilf's body so that it lay across the bed, the legs and head dangling either side.

He lay Sally on top of the body, face down with her stomach on Wilf's buttocks, forming a cross, Sally's raised arse being the centre.

Sally lay still and silent.

Julian rolled down her panties and tights and removed them. He lifted up her pretty dress and parted her slim thighs.

He lay down upon her, still besuited, only his fly zip open.

He nibbled her ear and reached for his penis.

Sally felt the thing slowly slide into her. She felt the gentle warm waves of womanhood sooth her tortured mind as Julian revolved and pressed and wriggled.

Sally moaned and sobbed and gasped and had the first orgasm of her life.

She felt love for the man who'd induced it.

Julian had felt her flood. Had heard the sighs.

He withdrew from the slushy rice-puddingy mess and pressed into the place he much preferred.

'Now it's my turn,' he whispered, as he stretched the tightness.

Sally pressed her hands to her head and tried to scream but couldn't. Then, slowly, she smiled.

Julian grunted with gratification.

Like an animal he pounded. .

Sally, Wilf, the bed, all shook beneath him.

The Boss, Tramp, Malcolm, Knuckles, Billy the Boot, and the Italian got out of the car.

'Get the sack,' ordered the Boss.

The Italian slunk to the rear of the car while the others made their way to the water.

'It's too shallow at the sides,' the Boss observed.

'Let's get a boat and dump it in the middle,' suggested Malcolm.

The Boss said, 'Good thinking,' and then snapped, 'Where is that punk?' and looked round to see the Italian struggling with the sack, trying desperately hard to catch them up.

They walked slowly, menacingly, the Boss slightly ahead.

Ordinary people, sitting quietly, uncomfortably in their deck chairs, had little idea of the evils perpetrated by these men.

Knuckles, in a panic-stricken voice, warned, 'Look out, Boss, a fed.'

They all saw the policeman walking toward them.

The Boss hissed, 'Look natural. Leave the talking to me.'

P.C. 83 stopped in his tracks and watched the group of men approach him. P.C. 83, a man of Ugandan descent, had been thinking about his imminent promotion to sergeant, and the nice house he was going to buy. Another few weeks at the increased overtime rate and he would be able to raise a mortgage. P.C. 83 felt contented.

'Afternoon, officer,' greeted the Boss.

'Afternoon, sir,' replied the policeman.

The Boss, sensing that the sack was receiving the policeman's puzzled glances, brought all his cunning to the fore. 'Feeding the ducks,' he said. 'Nice day, but getting a little chilly. Well, good day …'

P.C. 83 watched the group pass him.

It was a nice day and it was getting a little chilly. It was nearly knocking off time and there was curry for tea. A lot of work to do that night or he would never get his degree.

'Good day, sir,' said P.C. 83 smiling.

Tramp saw an old man lying on the grass, looking hungry and wretched.

Tramp went to the man and gave him a five pound note.

'Here you are, mate,' Tramp said.

'God bless you,' said the man.

Miss Plimsoll was freezing. She was covered in goose pimples and felt hungry.

She listened to the swishing of the tiny wavelets as they hit the concrete shore.

Miss Plimsoll's mother had been a keen swimmer. She had

taught all the children to swim before they were six. A remarkable woman who had played Chopin as well as she played tennis. A woman who would have all her husband's workers to lunch on Boxing-day and cope single-handed because she insisted that the kitchen staff should have a holiday too. What would she say if she knew that her little Evelyn had not found a man? Was she looking down from Heaven full of sadness because her daughter had faced the world alone?

Miss Plimsoll opened her eyes and rose from the towel she'd been lying on. Without really knowing why, she bounded to the water's edge and leaped in. The water swirled about her, cold and unfriendly.

A few people looked up from their papers and took in the sight of the lunatic woman in the water as she thrashed and splashed about as though it were the hottest day of summer. But the sight soon bored them and after a short while their eyes and their minds had turned to other things.

And Miss Plimsoll fought for, and caught, her breath. The water didn't seem so cold after all. She attacked the water with a powerful breast stroke.

Miss Plimsoll, if she wanted to, could swim the English Channel.

Malcolm's powerful biceps, for he was a rowing blue, pulled at the oars and sent the skiff skimming through the brown murkiness. The Boss sat at the fore of the craft and Knuckles and Billy the Boot weighted down the rear. Malcolm was remembering the day of his Boat Race and Billy the Boot was staring at P.C. 83 who was disappearing into the distance and Knuckles was giving his nails an oral manicure.

'Where's that bloody Eyetie?' demanded the Boss.

The Italian, peddling furiously, was propelling as best he could the small fibre-glass craft which was sitting dangerously low in the water, Tramp and the sack occupying the rear seat.

'Look at the fucker,' said the Boss. 'Bloody pitiful.'

Malcolm gave a grin and an extra hard pull.

Miss Plimsoll's eyes had caught sight of the two crafts and their strange occupants and sensed that all was not well. She watched the skiff stop and heard the funny little man give some instructions to the tired looking man who was working the cyclecraft.

Miss Plimsoll, her curiosity aroused and her sense of public duty shining like a beacon, ducked beneath the boundary marker of the lido and swam out, as quietly as she knew how, to the two boats.

Tramp stood up and the tiny craft rocked wildly. Knuckles and Billy the Boot found this amusing and laughed heartily until the Boss silenced them with a vicious glance.

Then the Boss said, 'All right, let's get it dumped.'

Tramp lifted the sack above his head.

'Gently, you fool,' hissed the Boss.

And Malcolm hid a frightened smile as Tramp gently lowered the sack into the water. He watched the gorilla of a man release the sack and watched it sink into its ignominious grave. The skeleton of Sambo; the bones of his old friend Adrian. Could Ad have, wondered Malcolm, ever, even in his wildest dreams, conceived of such an end?

'That's that then,' Miss Plimsoll heard the little man say.

And Miss Plimsoll dived down into the depths and felt for the sack. Her hands found the opening and delved inside.

Miss Plimsoll had a stout heart. She had spunk.

Miss Plimsoll brought out a bone.

She surfaced, tightly holding her discovery.

'Hey!' she shouted to the two escaping boats. 'Haven't you forgotten something!'

And she waved the white relic in the air.

'Stroik me pink!' shouted the Boss.

'Christ,' said Knuckles.

They stopped, and stared at the woman with horror. Miss Plimsoll returned their stare with a conceited smile.

Malcolm's first thought was that Miss Plimsoll was the Lady of the Boating Lake and, without instructions from the Boss, he rowed towards her, intent upon, like some latter-day Lancelot, plucking the proffered tibia from her goose-pimpled hand.

Miss Plimsoll was treading water gracefully and watched the boat approach her. She was the brave heroine hoodwinking the villains. She would receive a medal and be in the local paper and perhaps even meet the Prime Minister.

'Knock her bloody head off!' ordered the Boss.

The skiff got nearer and nearer to Miss Plimsoll.

'Faster, faster!' screamed the Boss.

Then something strange happened. Tramp bellowed, 'If you touch one 'air on 'er 'ead, I'll do for you, 'arper!!'

Malcolm stopped rowing out of amazement.

The Italian stopped peddling out of fear.

The Boss said quietly, 'What did you say?'

Tramp looked the Boss straight in the eye and said, 'You 'eard me.'

The Boss looked at Knuckles and Billy the Boot but said nothing.

The skiff was two feet away from where Miss Plimsoll was keeping herself afloat.

'Don't you want your bone back?' she asked, rather daringly.

The Boss frowned.

Tramp ordered the Italian to peddle up to the lady and on reaching her, he stretched out a huge tatooed arm and said, 'In you come, love.'

'But my clothes,' protested Miss Plimsoll.

She looked into Tramp's big eyes. She would be a missionary, fearlessly entering the savages' retreat. She would be the ace woman detective plunged into intrigue and adventure.

The bone slipped from her fingers and plopped back into the water.

'We'll fix you up with something,' said Tramp kindly.

So Miss Plimsoll's neat, cold, little body clamboured aboard with the assistance of Tramp. The Boss, Malcolm, Billy the Boot, Knuckles, and the Italian looked on with bewilderment.

The Boss, in an attempt to laugh the matter off, scoffed, 'The Tramp's in love. Hoo hoo hoo! The Tramp's found himself a tart.'

Miss Plimsoll felt a little embarrassed. But Tramp's arm was around her, warming her, protecting her. He had saved her life.

They all ignored the remark.

The Boss, fearing that Tramp was about to usurp his authority, said, 'Right. Anyone like a cigar?'

'Thanks, Boss,' said Knuckles gratefully.

'Cheers, Boss,' said Billy the Boot.

Malcolm took one too, wishing to stay on the winning side..
It was a good exercise in diplomacy.

'Righto, then,' chirped the Boss, more cheerfully. 'Row away.'

'Right, Boss,' said Malcolm.

They smoked cigars while the Italian pedalled and Tramp, one arm around Miss Plimsoll and another dangling in the water, thought how much his newly-found woman reminded him of Nancy.

They returned the boats and collected their deposits and made for the car.

Tramp and Miss Plimsoll sat in the back seat between Knuckles and Billy the Boot, and Malcolm sat at the front next to the Boss.

'Liverpool!' the Boss snapped at the Italian.

The Oldsmobile was started and moved off.

Miss Plimsoll was a little frightened but in her heart she knew that the kindly savage would protect her.

Malcolm felt a little ill at ease. He would remain loyal to the Boss as long as his authority lasted. When they were with Julian, Julian would take command. Of this, Malcolm was certain.

The Oldsmobile weaved through the London traffic.

It was the Boss who spoke first. He spat, 'Can't you drive any faster? We want to be there by today.'

The Italian took a deep breath. His heart-beat accelerated. So did the car.

Malcolm enquired, 'What are we going to do with Julian when we get there?'

The answer came from Tramp. 'I'm going to scoff 'im!'

Malcolm turned. 'Eat him? Whatever for?'

Tramp's voice faltered with emotion. 'He scoffed my kid.'

Malcolm looked downwards as a mark of respect. 'I see,' he said quietly.

Malcolm pondered on this. Eating Tramp's kid. It was hardly cricket.

Miss Plimsoll could hold her silence no longer. 'You mean you're all cannibals?' she gasped.

Tramp gave her a squeeze.

Miss Plimsoll thought she could feel her hair turning white. She longed for her little shop in Chelsea. She prayed that she would be whisked magically away to her cottage in the

Isle of Man. But nothing happened.

The car turned onto the motorway.

'Right!' screamed the Boss, 'Get the fucker moving!'

The Italian obeyed.

Malcolm longed for a safety belt and braced his feet against the bottom of the car.

The Oldsmobile streaked down the fast lane like a roller-coaster, belching out black smoke.

Tramp unzipped his fly and presented his fine upstanding organ.

Miss Plimsoll's intestines froze.

'Suck it, love,' said Tramp.

Miss Plimsoll looked at him, speechless, terrified.

'Go on, love, suck it,' pleaded the apeman.

Miss Plimsoll looked at his huge fists, she looked at Knuckles and Billy the Boot, she looked at the machine guns, she looked at the mammoth thing.

Tramp gave a grunt of impatience.

And Miss Plimsoll, feeling bilious, lowered her head and opened her tiny mouth. She closed her eyes tightly.

Tramp closed his eyes and let out an animal noise.

Knuckles and Billy the Boot discreetly looked away.

The Boss planned his strategy.

Malcolm produced adrenalin.

The Italian did his best to control the car.

And Miss Plimsoll desperately tried to retain the contents of her stomach.

Smith's dirty, long large toenail appeared through the hole in his sock that appeared through Smith's soleless shoe.

And Smith bounded down the concrete steps to his cave.

'Fucking cunting hell,' were the words he used to describe his failure to find his key.

Smith put his elbow through the glass in his door and stretched his hand through the jagged broken edges.

The door was open. He was safe.

He slammed the door and dived on the bed. He ached all over. His foot bore the impressions of countless thousands of small stones.

Smith reached for the bottle of whiskey that lay under the bed and pressed it to his foul-tasting mouth. He gulped. Rivulets of the stuff, not finding their mark, gouged a course through the grubby stubble and dripped onto the sheets.

'That's better,' said Smith.

He felt tired. He'd had a good day out. Except, that was, for his shoe falling to bits.

He closed his eyes and felt his head revolve slowly.

The bed was soft.

He took one more mouthful. Then he drained the almost empty bottle.

Smith's being glowed.

Tomorrow he would go to an Oxfam shop and get a new pair of shoes. They had good stuff. He would get ones with leather soles this time. Then his feet wouldn't sweat so much.

But the trouble with leather soles was that you weren't insulated if you trod on electric railway lines.

Smith thought.

Smith thought of Canada.

Of cine cameras.

Smith thought of seeing Grudge.

Julian laughed.

Sally walked from her stove to see what amused him.

'This is funny,' explained Julian, pointing at the television.

Julian laughed loudly.

'It for children,' scolded Sally. 'Not for grown men.'

Julian was getting hungry. 'Hurry it up, will you,' he said, not too unkindly.

Sally returned to the stove.

Julian laughed heartily.

He knew that soon he would have to return to the cockloft. He could always hide under Sally's bed, or go to a hotel with her, but he had promised himself the cockloft and the cockloft it would be.

Sally said, 'It hot,' as she passed the heaped plate to Julian.

He took it.

He ate it.

He said, 'It's getting cold in here.'

Sally rose from her meal, put a coin in the meter, and turned on the archaic gas fire.

Julian licked his plate and the fire hissed.

The fire hissed on and Julian's eyelids drooped.

Sally finished her meal, put the plate on the floor, and

sighed.
Julian placed his arm around her and pulled her nearer.
They sat and watched television.
Julian felt the softness of her skin.
The fire hissed.
Sally felt the secure warmth of strong arms.
Their stomachs were full.
In the cold room above lay the solitary figure of Wilf.

The Italian was beginning to feel groggy. So that Miss
Plimsoll would not catch her death of cold, Tramp had
turned the heater on full blast.
The Oldsmobile slowly veered across into the centre lane. A
lorry swerved and hooted wildly.
'Shite!!!' screamed the Boss.
Malcolm closed his eyes and pressed out his legs as hard as
he could.
The Italian steered back into the fast lane and rubbed his
eyes.
The Boss turned and nodded to Knuckles. Knuckles
reached in his pocket and brought out a penknife. He
selected the instrument used mostly for extracting stones
from horses' hooves and jabbed it into the back of the
Italian's neck.
The Italian screamed.
The car became temporarily out of control.
'Now concentrate,' warned the Boss.
Tramp was flying high.
Miss Plimsoll was getting used to it.
Billy the Boot was sleeping.
The Italian had a pain in the neck.
Knuckles stared out of the window.
'Have a cigar, Malcolm,' said the Boss.
'Thanks, Boss,' said Malcolm.

Smith rubbed his eyes. He'd been dreaming again. Smith
seemed to be dropping off and dreaming a lot lately. It
worried him a little.
He rose from the untidy bed and went towards the sink.
Outside, night was beginning to fall. Soon Smith would
have to go and see Grudge.
He splashed cold water over his face.

'Nyaahhhh!!' he uttered, and searched for a towel. He couldn't find one so he turned on the light. Naked, the bulb shone brightly, blindingly. A moth immediately flew towards it. Still wet-faced, Smith took hold of his good shoe and swatted at it like a man possessed. The moth darted and dodged but Smith's superior intellect won through and the fluttering creature soon lay crippled and helpless on the floor. Smith got an empty brandy bottle and managed to pour two or three droplets of the spirit onto the creature. Then he took his box of matches from the shelf by his sink and struck one. The chemical smell filled his nose and made him cough. Then Smith lowered the flaming vesta towards the damp dying insect saying, 'This is for all the times my Dad came home without a job and all the times I went hungry and …'

The match was burning Smith's fingers, so he did it. There was a small whoosh of flame.

Smith rubbed his eyes.

He was feeling hungry but he couldn't be bothered cooking anything.

He ransacked his food cupboard in search of biscuits and potato crisps.

Soon he would have to be making tracks.

Julian's tongue was inside Sally's ear.

Sally liked it.

Julian, sensing this, said, 'I'm going out for a walk.'

Sally looked a little cheated. 'I can come too?' she asked.

Julian shook his handsome head. 'No,' he said firmly and made for the door.

Sally sighed and turned the television back on.

Julian skipped down the uncarpeted stairs to the hallway. Letters in brown envelopes abounded. They all seemed to be marked 'Ministry of Health and Social Security' and addressed to people with unpronounceable names. Julian put them in his pocket and opened the front door.

Yellow lights shone above giving the street a depressing atmosphere.

Julian shivered a little and turned to his right.

He was conscious that his hands were thrust deep into his pockets and that his shoulders were hunched. He was slinking. He had become a slinker all of a sudden.

He walked.

And he walked.

Not really knowing where he was going, not knowing if he could find his way back.

He was cold and his breath was white smoke.

Julian looked around him. Just a few people at the top of the street. Nobody else.

He walked the twenty yards to where the small child played. Green snot encrusted its nose. It pushed a battered model car along.

Julian stood and watched it.

Looked around once more.

Said, 'Hello.'

The toddler looked up. Its face wore a smile.

Julian moved closer. 'Nice car you have.'

And then the smile on the face disappeared. Julian's hands had the toddler's neck in a strangulating grip. His blue eyes stared at the pain-wracked features.

His thumbs, perfectly formed, crushed into the infant's adam's apple.

The child shivered all over and sagged.

Julian released it and walked slowly away.

He stared at the lights above him.

'What now?' he asked himself. 'So what is new?'

Malcolm, at the Boss's request, turned on the car radio.

'Have another cigar,' said the Boss.

'Thanks, Boss,' said Malcolm.

The radio waffled out music.

The Italian was trying very hard not to feel groggy again.

Billy the Boot was asleep.

Knuckles was feeling car sick but was too ashamed to say anything, preferring to gulp ominously and then swallow every now and again.

Miss Plimsoll's mouth was getting tired and her tongue was numb.

Tramp, in a state of semi-euphoria, was considering the possibilities of buggering Miss Plimsoll over the back of the front seat.

The Boss's mind ticked over.

The miles melted away.

And Malcolm enjoyed his cigar.

Sally, thinking that the sound of footsteps coming up the stairs heralded Julian's return, got up from the couch and put the kettle on.

But the footsteps passed her door and continued upwards. There was a knock on Wilf's door and Sally listened, glad that they had locked it.

The knock came again and a voice said, 'Hello. Is there anybody in?'

Then came the pad clunk pad as Smith, with his soleless shoe, descended and breathed heavily with exhaustion outside Sally's door. Then he knocked.

Sally hesitated, then opened it.

She saw the sight that was Smith.

'Good evening,' said Smith very politely. 'My name is Mr. Smith and I don't suppose you could tell me the whereabouts of a Mr. Wilfred Grudge could you?' and Smith smiled as best he could.

Sally said, 'I think you better come in and wait for Julian.'

Smith entered and right away spotted the boiling kettle. His heart leaped.

'Would you like a cup of tea?' asked Sally.

'Yes please, miss,' said Smith, 'if it's not too much trouble.'

'No trouble,' said Sally.

And Smith, always on the lookout for new talent, mentally undressed her and liked what he saw.

When Julian returned, Smith and Sally were deep in conversation.

'What's going on?' he demanded.

'A discussion,' announced Smith, 'about the aesthetics of nude photography.'

'And rates of pay also,' said Sally.

Smith rose from the couch and extended his hand. 'You must be Julian.'

Julian looked at Smith's hand disdainfully and felt for his flick-knife.

'He came to see Wilf about some money,' explained Sally, fearing for Smith's safety.

'That's right,' said Smith. And then he added. 'Mr. Grudge often spoke of you with great pride.'

'For fuck's sake,' said Julian, taking out his wallet.

Smith caught sight of the fivers that nestled and said, 'About forty pounds, he owed me ...'

Julian detected the faltering optimism and grabbed Smith by the scruff of the neck.

'You scum,' said Julian coldly.

Smith was sent sprawling, then Julian threw a mug of hot tea over him.

Sally, fearing more violence, begged, 'No, darling ...'

She was interrupted as the door burst open.

'Yer fuckin' twat!!!' and suddenly Tramp had hold of Julian and was shaking him.

Sally and Smith and Malcolm and the Boss and Knuckles and Billy the Boot and Miss Plimsoll all watched with great interest as Tramp trapped Julian's left leg on the floor with his huge foot and heaved Julian's other leg in the air.

'Looks like a fuckin' wishbone don't he, Boss?' chuckled Tramp.

The Boss licked his thin lip rather nervously.

Julian's face was twisted with pain as Tramp demanded of him 'Make a fuckin' wish, then! Make a fuckin' wish ...!'

Malcolm gave the Boss a nudge and whispered in his ear.

The Boss whispered something in Tramp's ear and Julian was released.

The Boss said, 'Julian, my old friend. Malcolm tells me you have a father whom you love with all your heart. Would it not be fair, as you scoffed Tramp's son, if Tramp were to scoff your Dad?'

The small crowd waited, spellbound, for Julian's reply.

Malcolm was grinning and smoking yet another cigar.

Sally was confused and wanted to go to the toilet but was too scared.

Miss Plimsoll was staring into Julian's eyes.

Smith wished he had brought his camera.

Knuckles and Billy the Boot awaited orders.

The Boss schemed.

Julian smiled.

Tramp grunted.

And the Italian knocked and entered carrying a huge newspaper parcel and said, 'I got the fish and chips, Boss.'

'I think,' said Julian, rubbing his leg, 'that we should discuss this over a meal.'

Half an hour later, Wilf was in the boot of the Oldsmobile. The Italian, Billy the Boot, Knuckles, Sally, Miss Plimsoll, and Malcolm were in the back seat (Smith was lying on the floor); Tramp and the Boss were sprawled on the front seat; and Julian was driving them, very quickly, to his house in the country.

He was going to hold a party for them. It was all going to be all right.

Julian smiled to himself.

'Blind Harper for me, Tramp,' said Julian.

And Tramp leaned over, grabbed the ex-boss's small head, and rammed two mighty fingers into the small eye-sockets.

Joe Harper screamed and howled and was blind.

Tramp wiped iris and retina from his digits and smiled.

'Thanks, Alf,' said Julian.

'I say, Ju, it's a bit crowded back here,' said Malcolm. 'Could I borrow your knife?'

Julian, driving the old Oldsmobile very fast indeed, threw the knife over his shoulder.

'Thanks, Ju.'

Malcolm opened the knife and cut the Italian's throat.

Then he stabbed Sally through the heart.

Blood everywhere.

'You mean thing,' said Billy the Boot. 'I've never shagged a Chinawoman.'

'Nothing stopping him is there, Boss,' said Knuckles.

'No,' laughed Julian as the engine screamed out its power.

Miss Plimsoll, soaked in the Italian's blood, accidentally trod on Smith's face.

'Sorry,' she said, vomiting all over Billy the Boot's shirt.

Tramp said, 'If you want Evie to suck your dick, Boss, it's all right with me.'

'Thanks,' said Julian with a grin, 'but no thanks.'

And Julian indicated, braked, and turned into a motorway café.

'We'll stop here,' he said, 'to dump the bodies and have a bite to eat.'

'Yes, Boss,' came the chorus.

The sun was rising when Julian steered the battered car into the driveway of his neo-Georgian mansion. A blackbird was singing.

'Put him over there, boys,' directed Julian. 'Hang him up

by the legs next to the others.'
Billy the Boot and Knuckles dragged Wilf's body to the wrack from which the putrid bodies of two unfortunate and forgotten children were hanging. They held their breath as they carried out their instructions, then, not speaking, they followed Julian up the cellar stairs.

After a hearty breakfast, Julian performed a marriage ceremony for Alf Tramp and Evelyn. Mrs. Tramp cried, for she knew that she would never marry Julian.
And Alf cried with joy when he thought of the fine son his new wife would bear him.
Joe Harper, wearing sunglasses that once belonged to the Italian, made plans for the party.
Julian and Malcolm cuddled each other in Julian's four-poster bed.
Billy the Boot and Knuckles got drunk on good brandy.
And Smith lay on the Persian carpet and thought of his Dad.
Smith had never felt happier.
And the sun shone brightly that day.

And in the dark, foul-smelling cellar, Wilf regained consciousness.
He thought briefly of Howard.
Then he wished he was in Liverpool.
'Sod it,' he whispered.
Then died.